GOTCHA!

Speaking and Listening Activities for Intermediate Learners

ALYSSA MATUCK
AND
YASMIN I. VALI

Dominie Press, Inc.

Acknowledgments

The authors would like to thank Jim Beasley, Bob Betts, Bill Brechtel, and especially Aram Adlparvar, Nathan Aminian, Ken Baumheckel, Joe Bergman, Peter Cassidy, Cecily Chaffee, Catherine Condon, Shawn Hutchens, Safineh Tahmassebi, John Thomas, David Urbina, Farrah Vali, Nadeah Vali, and the studios of KUCI 88.9 in Irvine, California for their help in recording the audiocassette to accompany *Gotcha!*

Publisher: Raymond Yuen
Executive Editor: Carlos Byfield
Editorial Assistant: Bob Rowland
Designer: Gary Hamada
Illustrator: E. Silas Smith

Published by:

Dominie Press, Inc.
1949 Kellogg Avenue
Carlsbad, California 92008 USA

ISBN 1-56720-872-4
Printed in Singapore by PH Productions.

2 3 4 5 6 11 10 09

This book is dedicated to:

George C. Matuck
Leslie D. Theroux
J. David Urbina

and

Fazlu and Shamsuddin
I. Val Vali
Nadeah, Farrah, and Mathian Shaafi Vali

Table of Contents

To the Learner

Gotcha! was written to help you improve your conversation, listening, speaking, and vocabulary skills. After using this book, you will be able to discuss various topics and use vocabulary related to those topics. The text will also help you improve some grammar and pronunciation skills. In addition, you will better understand American culture, and be more prepared to discuss your own culture, as well.

There are 12 units in *Gotcha!*, along with an audiocassette to accompany the dialogues and listening activities. We have included a variety of activities throughout the book to make it interesting.

Each unit contains the following features:

- **Brainstorming:** Introduces the dialogue with an illustration or illustrations followed by questions. It is designed to stimulate interest in the dialogue and allow you to bring to the task any background knowledge and/or experience you might have of the topic.
- **Vocabulary, Idioms, and Expressions:** Introduces the vocabulary, common idioms, and expressions to be used in the unit, and gives you listening practice through note-taking.
- **Prelistening:** Introduces questions that get you thinking about the topics and/or cultural aspects of the dialogues.
- **Dialogue:** A realistic dialogue with a surprise or unexpected ending. It presents vocabulary, pronunciation, and/or grammar points to be used in the unit as well as aspects of American culture for discussion.
- **Comprehension Questions:** Includes factual and inferential questions designed to ensure that you understand any implied nuances of the dialogue.
- **Language Focus:** Either presents a grammar or a pronunciation point that is also presented in the dialogue. It also provides an activity to practice the structure or pronunciation point.
- **Vocabulary Activities:** Offers an opportunity for you to actively use the vocabulary, idioms, and expressions in different contexts.
- **Speaking Activities:** Offers extensive practice in fluency development as well as reinforcement of vocabulary from previous sections.
- **Listening Activities:** Includes task-based listening activities based on various types of realistic listening (interviews, comprehension questions, talk shows, conversations, telephone messages, news accounts, etc.).

Speaking and listening skills are essential to learning a foreign language. We hope that this book will make this learning process an enjoyable one for you.

To the Teacher

Gotcha! is a listening and speaking skills textbook and accompanying audiocassette designed for intensive language programs, adult ESL programs, and community colleges. We decided to write this textbook after several frustrating attempts teaching courses in oral and aural skills. We found ourselves pulling from various sources and texts in order to meet the objectives of our course. It is our aim to meet both speaking and listening objectives of a course in one text. The number and type of activities and lessons in the book are extensive enough so that creating additional lessons and using other sources are kept to a minimum. We have included realistic dialogues (each containing a surprise ending, which is why we chose the title *Gotcha!*) which are accompanied by listening comprehension questions that ensure students understand the implied nuances of the conversation as well as its facts. These dialogues also present new vocabulary that students can use in the vocabulary-building activities. Also included in the text are: speaking activities to promote fluency, task-based listening activities, grammar lessons, and pronunciation activities. Another element other texts seemed to neglect that we have included in our text, is variety. Although each unit contains the same sections, each activity within the sections is different throughout the book. This is sure to capture the interest of the learners, and at the same time lend some structure to the teacher. It also helps learners with different learning styles to benefit from the text.

Finally, we have provided learners with enticing and relevant topics with which to learn English. Each unit revolves around a different topic. Because of the rich variety and quantity of the activities, it may not be possible to complete the entire text in one quarter or semester; learners and instructors can choose those topics that are most interesting to their class.

We hope that you enjoy teaching from this text. We encourage you to refer to the teacher's manual for specific suggestions, guidance, answer keys, tapescripts, and tests. Please note that some activities in the text **require** the use of the teacher's manual and tapes. The unit tests, which are found in the *Gotcha! Teacher's Manual,* evaluate students' understanding of vocabulary from the unit, and offer a final assessment of listening on the topic presented in the unit. The listening portions of the tests are on a separate audiocassette.

Dating and Marriage

Brainstorming

Look at the two pictures below. Read and answer these questions:

Picture 1. What are these two people doing? What is their relationship to each other? What are they saying to each other? How do they feel?

Picture 2. Who is this man? What is his relationship to the woman? Where are they? What are they talking about? How do they feel?

Vocabulary, Idioms, and Expressions

Practice pronouncing the following list of words and expressions. Then, take notes while your teacher gives the definitions.

Vocabulary

matchmaker
to propose
anniversary
amazing
romantic
engaged
doubt
timing
dating service
wedding ceremony
aisle
best man
bridesmaid
flower girl
ring bearer
superstition
divorce
compatible

Idioms and Expressions

to thank someone enough
How does that sound?
to fall in love
to get cold feet
second thoughts
to go through with something
to set (someone) up
made for each other
to get along with

Dialogue

Prelistening

Discuss the following questions.

1. How do couples usually meet in your country?
2. Why do people decide to get married? When do they know they have found the right person?
3. Who usually proposes marriage?
4. How does a man or woman propose?
5. What is a wedding ceremony in your country like?
6. Are the bride and groom usually nervous before the ceremony? Why?

Dialogue

Listen to the following dialogue with your books closed. Take notes as you listen, so you can ask your teacher any questions you may have.

CAST OF CHARACTERS

MARCO
ANGELINA
SERGIO

Marco: I can't thank you enough for introducing me to Angelina. She is the best thing that has ever happened to me.

Sergio: That's great.

Marco: Really, Sergio. You're a great matchmaker.

Sergio: Yeah, I know.

Marco: I've been thinking about proposing to her. What do you think of that?

Sergio: Oh, I'm really happy for you two.

Marco: The only problem is that I'm real nervous. What if she says no?

Sergio: I'm sure she'll say yes. What woman wouldn't? You're handsome, rich, and romantic. I have to go, Marco. It's getting late.

(A few days later, Marco and Angelina are on a beautiful boat. There is moonlight shining on the water, and a man is playing the violin. It is very romantic.)

Marco: I have to talk to you about something very important.

Angelina: So do I. It's my parents' 25th wedding anniversary. They're having a party. I'd like you to come over to our house so you can meet them.

Marco: They have been married for 25 years? That's amazing.

Angelina: The party is next Saturday at 7 o'clock. I'll pick you up at 6. How does that sound?

Marco: Okay. I guess.

Angelina: What did you want to talk about?

Marco: Uhhh ... I just want to tell you how much you mean to me. You know, I think I fell in love with you the first time I met you. And now, you have become such a big part of my life. Will you marry me?

Angelina: You're so romantic, you want to be engaged! But didn't you forget something?

Marco: Oh yeah! I almost forgot. Here's the ring. Will you marry me?

Angelina: I don't know what to say. This is the most beautiful ring I've ever seen. Okay, sure. I love the ring... Oh, and of course I love you, too. Yes! Yes! I'll marry you.

(Several months later, Marco and Angelina's wedding ceremony is about to begin.)

Marco: I'm really nervous. Sergio, I think I'm getting cold feet. I really love Angelina, but I hope that I will always feel that way about her.

Sergio: What do you mean? Are you having second thoughts?

Marco: Isn't that normal?

Sergio: Come on, Marco. We have to go now. The ceremony is starting.

Marco: I feel sick, Sergio. I'm serious. I don't know if I can go through with this. Could you talk to Angelina for me?

Sergio: I can't believe this is happening!

(In Angelina's dressing room)

Sergio: Angelina, I have to talk to you.

Angelina: Right now? The wedding is just about to begin.

Sergio: Marco is having a few doubts.

Angelina: What are you saying?

Sergio: He can't go through with the marriage. But, Angelina, I have something else I've been wanting to tell you for a long time. I know this isn't the best timing. But, I have been in love with you for about five years. I only set you up with Marco because I didn't think you would ever love me.

Angelina: Oh, Sergio.

Comprehension

Answer the following questions without looking back at the dialogue. If necessary, listen to the dialogue again.

1. What is the best thing that has ever happened to Marco?
2. Why is Marco amazed that Angelina's parents have been married for 25 years?
3. Why doesn't Angelina answer Marco's proposal right away?
4. Why doesn't Sergio try to change Marco's mind when he has doubts about getting married?
5. How do you think Angelina feels when she hears that Marco can't go through with the wedding?
6. How do you think she feels when she hears that Sergio is in love with her?
7. What do you think will happen to Marco, Angelina, and Sergio in the future?

Language Focus

Read and Study

The present progressive is used to talk about actions that are happening now, right now, at this moment. Examples of expressions used with the present progressive include: **these days, currently, today, at the present, this week, this year, this month.** The present progressive is formed by using **am, is, are (to be verb)** and an **-ing** form of an action verb. Look at the present progressive verbs used in the dialogue.

Subject	+	**be verb**	+	**-ing form of "action" verb**	+	**(object)**
1. It	+	is	+	getting	+	late.
2. I	+	am	+	getting	+	cold feet.
3. Marco	+	is	+	having	+	a few doubts.

Language Focus Activity 1

Fill in the blanks with the correct -ing form of the verbs listed below.

play throw wear wait take

1. The bride_______________ such a beautiful dress.
2. The flower girl _______________ rose petals down the aisle of the church.
3. Lorena _______________ for her boyfriend to pick her up.
4. The band _______________ our song.
5. The limousine _______________ the couple to the hotel.

Language Focus Activity 2

Answer the following questions orally.

1. Watch your teacher doing several different things. What is she or he doing?
2. What classes are you taking this semester/quarter?
3. Are you participating in any clubs or on any sports teams currently? Explain.
4. Are you doing anything special this week/month/year? Explain.

Vocabulary Activities

Vocabulary Activity 1 CONCENTRATION

1. Behind some squares, there are sentences with missing words. Behind other squares, there are vocabulary words.
2. Choose two squares. **Example:** 2 and 36. Your teacher will read what is behind each square. If one is a vocabulary word and the other one is its matching sentence, you get a point for that match. If they are not a match, then the other team gets to take a turn. Keep choosing squares until all 18 matches have been found.

1	2	3	4	5	6
7	8	9	10	11	12
13	14	15	16	17	18
19	20	21	22	23	24
25	26	27	28	29	30
31	32	33	34	35	36

Vocabulary Activity 2 GOOD AND BAD EXAMPLES

1. Circle the items below that cannot be **proposed.**

some money	a toast	an idea
a joke	a plan	marriage

2. Circle the activities that a **flower girl** would not do during a wedding.

cry	throw flower petals	dance
carry a ring	eat cake	help the bride get ready

3. Circle the things below that are not **amazing**.

birth	man on the moon	brushing hair
computers	sleeping	falling in love

4. Circle the examples of bad **timing** below.

   You catch all green lights on the road.

   You're in the shower when the phone rings.

   A big bird flies over your car right after you have washed it.

   You are on a coffee break when your boss comes to talk to you.

   Your friend is mad at you and you need a favor from him or her.

   You turn the radio on, and your favorite song is playing.

5. Circle the common reasons why people **divorce.**

   Only one person wants children.

   They handle money differently.

   They have an affair.

   One person forgot to take out the trash.

   One person comes home late most of the time.

   One person has bad teeth.

Speaking Activities

Speaking Activity 1 DATING INTERVIEW

Interview a native English speaker and complete the following survey about dating and marriage. Then, share the results with the class.

1. At what age did you start dating?
2. Would you go, or have you gone, on a blind date?
3. Who usually pays on a date, the man or the woman?
4. Describe the best date you've ever had.
5. Describe the worst (or the most embarrassing) date you've ever had.
6. Would you use a dating service?
7. How important is it to you that your partner have a good education?
8. Would you marry someone from a different culture? Why or why not?
9. Would you live with your girlfriend or boyfriend before getting married? Explain.
10. Would you consider marrying someone with children? Explain.
11. Ask American couples to describe their marriage proposals.
12. Ask your own question.

Speaking Activity 2 YOUR IDEAL PARTNER

Divide into two groups, preferably men on one side, women on the other. With your group, make a list of qualities and traits you look for in a partner. Then, write the 10 most important qualities. Discuss similarities and differences in each group's expectations.

A woman's ideal partner should be:	A man's ideal partner should be:
1.	1.
2.	2.
3.	3.
4.	4.
5.	5.
6.	6.
7.	7.
8.	8.
9.	9.
10.	10.

Speaking Activity 3 SINGLES' ADS

1. Write a singles' ad and give it to the teacher.
2. The following day, the teacher will give you a copy of all personal ads, without names on them.
3. Divide into groups of three and guess who wrote each of the personal ads.

Describe yourself	Describe the kind of person you are looking for
1. Age or approximate age	1. Age or approximate age
2. Hobbies and interests	2. Hobbies and interests
3. Appearance	3. Appearance
4. Occupation	4. Occupation
5. Other	5. Other

Speaking Activity 4 DATING SERVICE

You and your group members are employees of the "Singles Connection," a dating service. Read the descriptions of the following eight single people (four women and four men) and try to match each man with a woman. Discuss why you made your matches.

1. Hee-Sook Lee

Age: 25 years
Appearance: Silky, long black hair, 5 feet tall, 100 pounds, beautiful, tanned skin
Marital Status: Single, never married
Occupation: Nurse
Hobbies: Swimming, water-skiing, going to the beach
Statement: I want to find a good-looking, rich doctor who wants to have fun. I want a man who likes outdoor activities.

2. Chi-Huang Tsai

Age: 38 years
Appearance: Handsome, with shoulder-length hair; sometimes wear a ponytail
Marital Status: Divorced with no children
Occupation: Owner/Manager of a night club
Hobbies: Like fast cars, music, and dancing
Statement: I am looking for an attractive, fun-loving woman. I just want to have a good time.

3. Sibel Sen

Age: 31 years
Appearance: Tall and slender, with wavy, light brown hair
Marital Status: Divorced with a child
Occupation: Architect
Hobbies: Cooking and baking, camping
Statement: I am looking for a friendly, outgoing man with a good sense of humor. He must like children and the outdoors.

4. Isao Oshima

Age: 24 years
Appearance: Tall and muscular, with short black hair
Marital Status: Single, never married

Occupation: Karate instructor
Hobbies: Working out, entering "Muscle Man" contests, and riding motorcycles
Statement: I would like to find an experienced, older woman.

5. Francois Bazus

Age: 27 years
Appearance: Green-blue eyes, tall and slender
Marital Status: Single, never married
Occupation: 4th-year biology student
Hobbies: Love camping
Statement: I want to have a relationship with a beautiful woman. I want to share some of my hobbies with her.

6. Faisal Al-Beibi

Age: 37 years
Appearance: Wavy black hair
Marital Status: Divorced with two children
Occupation: Accountant
Hobbies: Horseback riding and hunting
Statement: I am looking for a woman who would like to be a part of my family.

7. Christina Gonzales

Age: 40 years
Appearance: Long brown hair and light brown eyes
Marital Status: Single, never been married
Occupation: Disc jockey
Hobbies: Playing guitar and traveling
Statement: I want to travel to different cities and have fun with my man. I don't want children.

8. Huong Nguyen

Age: 32 years
Appearance: Petite, with shoulder-length hair
Marital Status: Single
Occupation: Works in a beauty salon
Hobbies: Fashion design and shopping
Statement: I would like to have a relationship with an athletic man.

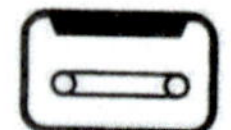

Listening Activity

CLOZE PASSAGE

Listen to the following passage and fill in the missing words.

Sam and Jin-Sook are a handsome ________________. Jin-Sook's friend, Lucy, says that they are ________________. They had their 10th ________________last year. Their marriage has had its share of ________________, but they have solved their marital problems by going to a marriage counselor. He advised them to ________________ their misunderstandings. They followed his advice of not only ________________, but also ________________. Now they can't ________________ each other's company. Lucy ________________ them all the time. She says that they look like ________________ who have just returned from their ________________.

Questions

Write answers to the questions you hear.

1. ____

____

2. ____

____

3. ____

____

4. ____

____

Food and Restaurants

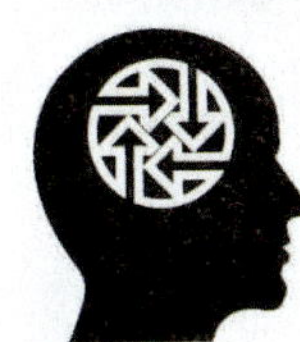

Brainstorming

Look at the picture below. Read and answer these questions:

Who are these people? What are they doing? Why are they there? How is the man feeling? How is the woman feeling? Why do they feel differently?

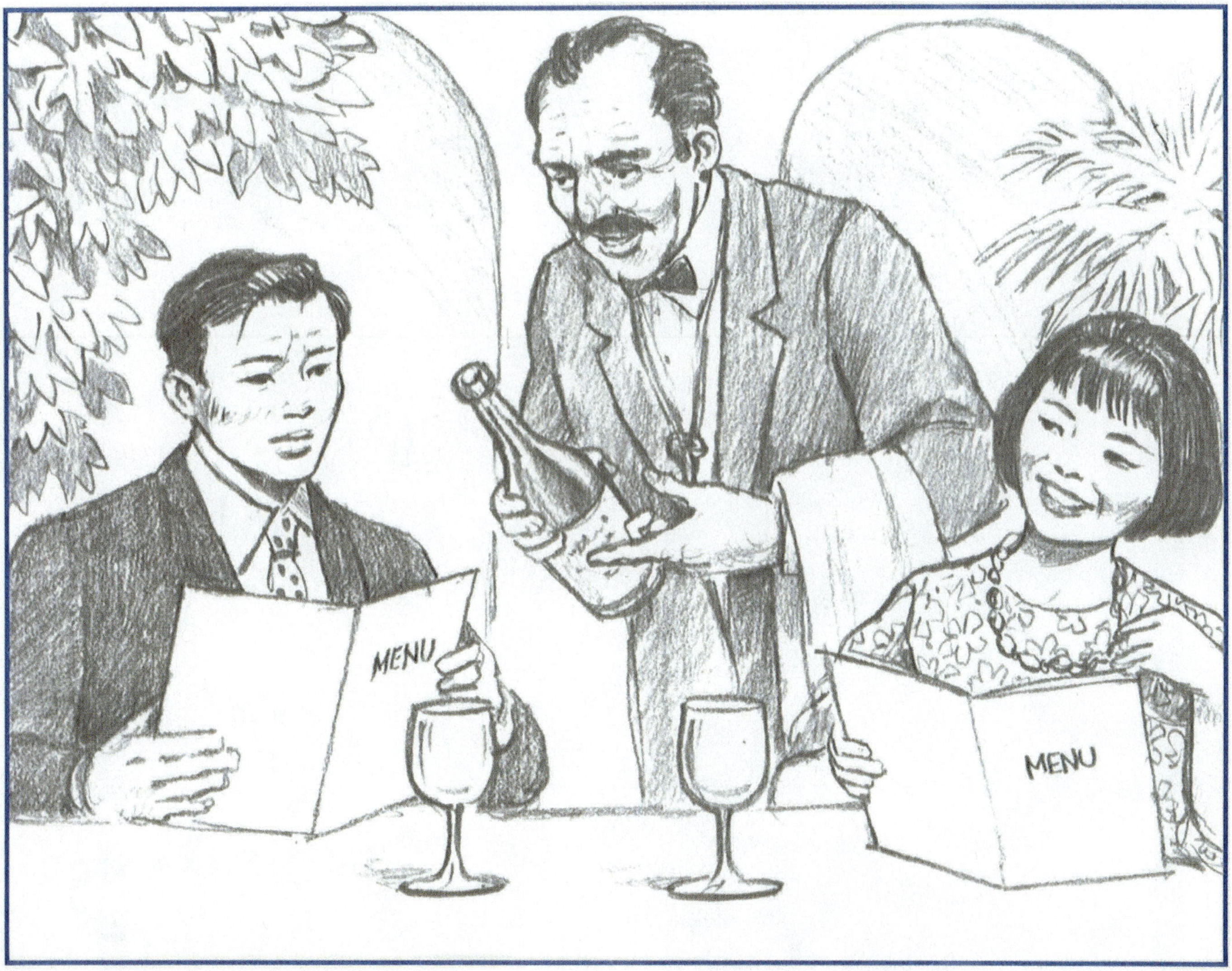

Vocabulary, Idioms, and Expressions

Practice pronouncing the following list of words and expressions. Then, take notes while your teacher gives the definitions.

Vocabulary

fancy
starved/starving
to taste/ to try
main course
appetizer
oysters
nutritious
junk food
lately
vegetarian
homemade
dessert
recipe
ingredients
snack
appetite
manners/etiquette
to stir
silverware
brunch
entree
buffet
to tip
to sip

Idioms and Expressions

to be high in
to set or clear the table
to go out
to have a bite
to start you off with
to be broke
on a diet
to be full
eating for two
Gees
to zap

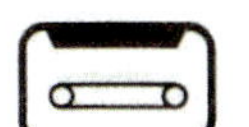

Dialogue

Prelistening

Discuss the following questions.

1. When you go out to a fancy restaurant in your country, what kinds of food do you order?
2. What do you typically order for an appetizer?
3. What kinds of foods do you eat when you're on a diet?
4. Do fancy restaurants in your country have dress codes?

Dialogue

Listen to the following dialogue with your books closed. Take notes as you listen, so you can ask your teacher any questions you may have.

CAST OF CHARACTERS

KATSU **JUNKO**

WAITER **HOST**

(Junko and her husband, Katsu, are at a fancy American restaurant.)

Katsu: Table for two, please.

Host: Okay, this way please. Our special today is swordfish cooked in white wine and garlic.

Junko: That sounds good. I'm starved.

(After a few minutes)

Junko: Well, I think I'm going to try the special.

Katsu: I'm not sure what I'm going to have as a main course. Let's start with an appetizer. I'd like to have fresh oysters. What about you?

Junko: Okay. I read in a magazine that oysters are really nutritious. They're high in iron.

Katsu: I can't believe you're concerned about your health. That's unusual for you.

Junko: I know. I eat too much junk food.

(The waiter comes.)

Waiter: Good evening. Could I start you off with an appetizer, or a bottle of wine?

Katsu: Oh, I love white wine. What kinds do you have?

Waiter: We have “Michael Mondi” and “Cruz Creek.” They both would go well with any fish.

Katsu: Okay, we’ll have a bottle of “Cruz Creek” and a dozen oysters.

Waiter: Very good.

Junko: I love going out. We should do this more often.

(The waiter returns with a bottle of wine.)

Waiter: Here you go. Would you like to taste it, sir?

Katsu: Sure. It’s fine, thank you.

(The waiter begins to serve Junko a glass of wine.)

Junko: I’m not having any wine. Thank you.

Katsu: Really? What’s the matter with you? You told me you loved white wine. Can I please have a glass of water, too?

Waiter: Yes, of course. Have you decided on the main course?

Junko: Yes, I have. I’m going to have the special, and a glass of orange juice, please.

Katsu: I’m on a diet. Do you have anything vegetarian?

Waiter: Yes, we have a delicious pasta dish mixed with eggplant, broccoli, and carrots.

Katsu: Okay, I’ll try that.

Waiter: Would you like a dinner salad with that?

Katsu: No, I don’t think so.

Junko: Oh, I’ll have one with blue cheese dressing. How long will the oysters take? I’m so hungry. Could I have some bread while I’m waiting?

Waiter: The oysters will be out in about five minutes. I’ll bring some bread right away.

Katsu: Honey, relax. You’re embarrassing me. When did you have lunch?

Junko: I had a burger and fries at about three today.

Katsu: Gees, that was a couple of hours ago. I can’t believe you’re this hungry!

(The waiter serves bread and oysters.)

Junko: These are tasty.

Katsu: They sure are!

(After some time, the waiter serves the main course.)

Junko: This is absolutely wonderful. I have to get the recipe. How's your pasta? Can I have a bite?

Katsu: I haven't had a chance to taste it yet.

Junko: I'm sorry. I don't mean to be so rude. It just looks so delicious.

(15 minutes later)

Junko: That was tasty. What's for dessert?

Katsu: Gosh! I'm full. How can you think of eating anything else?

Junko: Honey, I have something to tell you. I'm so hungry because I'm eating for two.

Katsu: What do you mean? We are having a baby! I can't believe it.

Junko: So, please, can I enjoy a piece of homemade pie?

Katsu: Of course. Waiter!

Comprehension

Answer the following questions without looking back at the dialogue. If necessary, listen to the dialogue again.

1. In what kind of a restaurant are Junko and Katsu dining?
2. Why does Junko want to order oysters?
3. Why is Katsu surprised when Junko explains why she wants to order oysters?
4. How many oysters does Katsu order?
5. How many courses does Junko order? What are they?
6. Why does Junko apologize to Katsu after asking to taste his dinner?
7. Why does she have a big appetite?

Language Focus

Read and Study

A reduction is a blending or mixing of sounds, or a dropped sound in spoken English. Reductions occur more frequently when the context is informal. Commonly reduced words include: articles, prepositions, conjunctions, helping verbs, pronouns, and forms of the verb "to be." Also, when a **[t]** sound falls between two vowels, it becomes a **[d]** sound. Some other words naturally blend together by dropping sounds (see below). Look at and practice pronouncing the following examples of reductions from the dialogue.

Articles

Let's start with an appetizer. ➜ Let's start with n appetizer.

Prepositions

Table for two. ➜ Table fer two.
A bottle of wine. ➜ A bottle a wine.

Conjunctions

Cooked in white wine and garlic. ➜ Cooked in white wine n garlic.

Helping Verbs

What kinds do you have? ➜ What kinds dya have?

Can I please have a glass of water? ➜ Cin I please have a glass of water?
When did you have lunch? ➜ When dja have lunch?

Pronouns

Here you go. ➜ Here ya go.

Forms of "to be"

I'm going to try.... ➜ I'm gonna try....
We're going to have a baby. ➜ We're gonna have a baby.

T ➜ D

I had a burger and fries at about three o'clock. ➜ I had a burger and fries ad about three.

Other blending words

What do you mean? ➜ Whaddya mean?
How can you think of eating? ➜ How cin ya think of eatin?
Would you like to taste it? ➜ Woodya likta taste it?

Language Focus Activity

Write the long form of the reductions your teacher reads. Then practice pronouncing the reduced form.

1. ______________________________

2. ______________________________

3. ______________________________

4. ______________________________

5. ______________________________

Vocabulary Activities

Vocabulary Activity 1 HIT OR MISS

1. Divide the class into two groups, with students standing in two lines.
2. The first student in each line is given a fly swatter or a feather duster.
3. Then, the teacher reads the definition of the vocabulary word. The students in the front with the fly swatters or dusters figure out what the word is and hit the word card. Whoever hits it first gets a point for the group.
4. Repeat this process for each of the vocabulary words.

Vocabulary Activity 2 BUILDING SENTENCES

1. Divide the class into four groups: A, B, C, and D.
2. Give each group one set of words.
3. The students ask native English speakers for sentences for their vocabulary words, and then bring the sentences to class and share them with the other three groups.

Group A	Group B
fancy	junk food
to start off with	to go out
manners/etiquette	silverware
oyster	homemade
on a diet	eating for two
to set the table	snack
lately	entree
ingredients	specialty
brunch	dessert
Group C	**Group D**
to tip/tip	nutritious
main course	buffet
to be full	to have a bite
to be high in something	to zap
recipe	appetite
starved	to sip
to be broke	to stir
appetizer	to taste/to try
to clear the table	vegetarian

Speaking Activities

Speaking Activity 1A TABLE MANNERS

The people in the illustrations on the next page are displaying bad American table manners. With a partner, discuss what is wrong in each picture and what the person should be doing. Be prepared to give the answers to the class.

Speaking Activity 1B DISCUSSION

Discuss one difference between table manners in the United States and table manners in your country.

Speaking Activity 2 ADJECTIVE GAME

1. Group students into three or four teams.
2. The teacher calls out adjectives. Then, each team brainstorms and comes up with as many food items as possible for each adjective.
3. The team that produces the most original answers wins the round.

Example: soggy — cereal that has been in milk for a long time.

salty	sweet
crunchy	bitter
sour	rich
chewy	sticky
spicy	mushy
bland	creamy
messy	juicy
stale	soggy
hot	cold

Speaking Activity 3 PACKAGED FOOD

1. **Bring your favorite canned or packaged food to class for discussion.**
2. **In groups, discuss your food item. The following questions are things you might want to discuss.**

1. When do you eat this food?
2. How often do you eat this food?
3. How is it prepared?
4. Why is this your favorite packaged food?
5. Can you describe your food, using any of the adjectives in this chapter?
6. Is your food nutritious, or is it considered junk food?

Speaking Activity 4 WHAT DO YOU SAY?

Make appropriate responses to the following questions and statements. There may be more than one correct answer.

QUESTIONS/STATEMENTS	RESPONSES
How would you like your steak cooked?	
How do you want your eggs?	
Would you like soup or a salad with your entree?	
What dressing would you like on your salad?	
What can I get you tonight?	
How is your meal?	
Can I get you anything else?	
Wow! That looks good.	
Where did you learn to cook? This is very good.	

What other questions/statements have you heard about food and restaurants? How did you respond?

Questions/Statements	Responses

Speaking Activity 5 FOOD BUDGET

1. Bring a menu from your favorite restaurant to class.
2. Divide the class into groups.
3. Each group has a budget to spend on an outing to a restaurant. The group chooses a restaurant that is economical and has good food. Members of the group plan the items that they will order and calculate the total cost, including the tip.
4. The groups report about their plan and budget to the class. The class will then judge which group was the most economical in planning their budget.

CULTURAL QUESTION: Do you tip food servers in your country? How much? Do you tip any other groups of people who provide you with a service?

Budget:
Items ordered and Prices:

Tax:
Tip:
Total Cost:
Money Left Over:

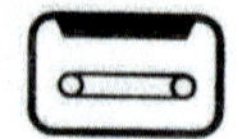

Listening Activities

Listening Activity 1 RADIO ADVERTISEMENT

Listen to the following radio advertisement about restaurants.

Then answer the questions that follow.

1. What are the two types of restaurants being advertised?

QUESTIONS	MEXICAN	CHINESE
Which restaurant has a lunch special?		
In which restaurant do you need to leave a tip?		
If you were really hungry, which restaurant would you go to?		

Listening Activity 2 TEACHER'S FAVORITE RECIPES

Listen while your teacher explains how to make two of his or her favorite foods. Take notes below. Then, summarize the recipes for a classmate, using your notes. Does your classmate agree with your summary?

Ingredients: ______________________________

____

Step 1: ______________ Step 8: ______________

Step 2: ______________ Step 9: ______________

Step 3: ______________ Step 10: ______________

Step 4: ______________ Step 11: ______________

Step 5: ______________ Step 12: ______________

Step 6: ______________ Step 13: ______________

Step 7: ______________ Step 14: ______________

Emotions, Feelings, and Moods

Brainstorming

Look at the picture below. Read and answer these questions:

Where are these people? How are these people feeling? Why are they feeling this way?

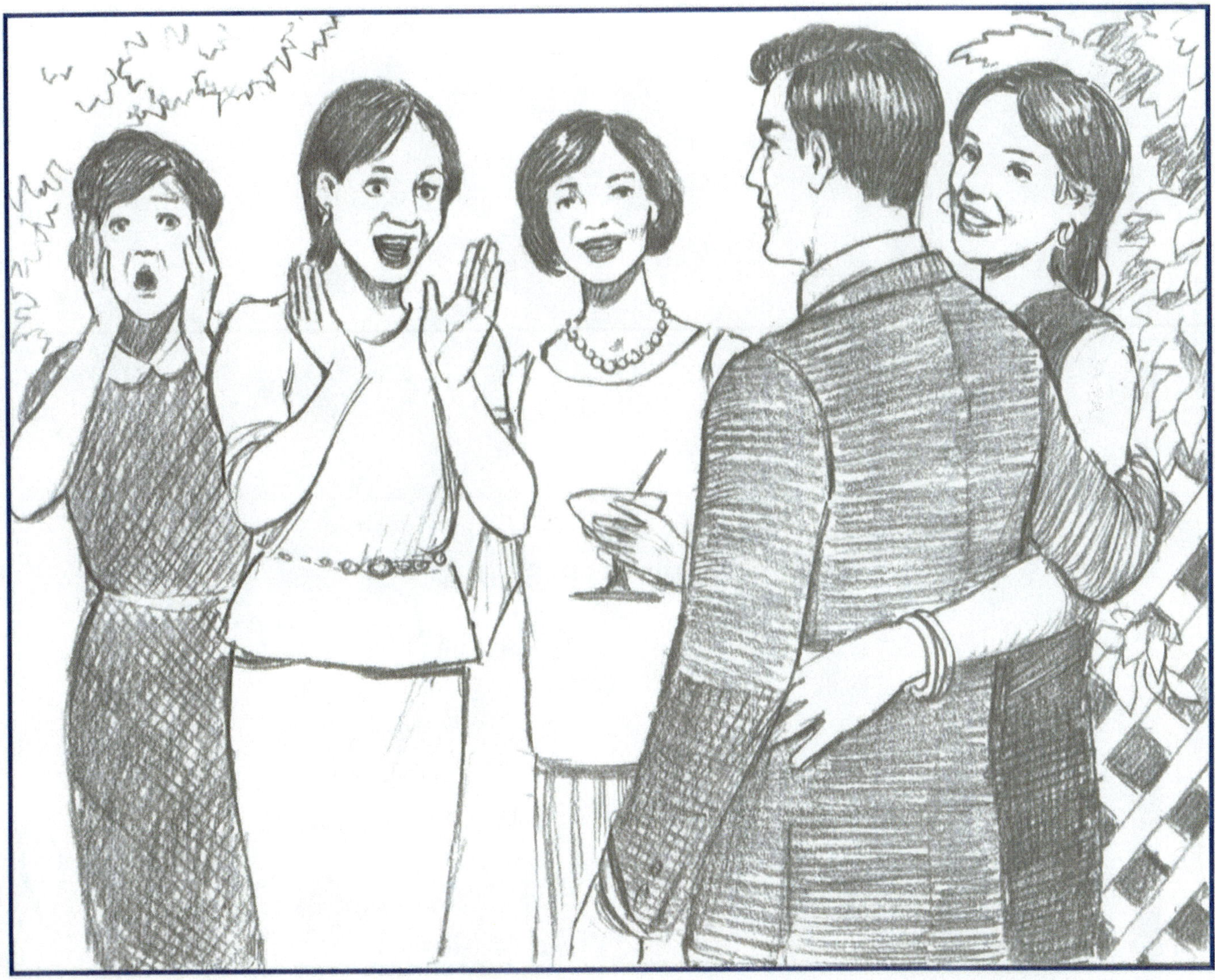

Vocabulary, Idioms, and Expressions

Practice pronouncing the following list of words and expressions. Then, take notes while your teacher gives the definitions.

Vocabulary

bitter
thrilled
confused
depressed
nervous
surprised
shocked
exhausted
terrified
horrible
frustrated
curious
terrible
grateful
satisfied
content
relaxed
jealous
regretful
lonely
to yell
excited
anxious

Idioms and Expressions

pooped
to be scared to death
to be on cloud nine
to feel (or look) like a million bucks
to have feelings for somebody
to loosen up
to be about to drop dead
to be shaking like a leaf
to be, or feel, down
to lose one's temper
to scream (or yell) at the top of one's lungs
Gees
You'll never guess
to be in a ______________ mood
You guys
to drive someone crazy
to calm down
opposites attract

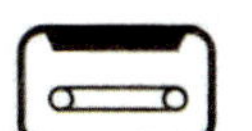

Dialogue

Prelistening

Discuss the following questions.

1. Do you have class reunions in your country?
2. If you do, how do you feel right before you go to the reunion? If you don't, ask someone about his or her class reunion.
3. If you have been to a class reunion, share your experience. Did anything unexpected happen? How did you feel? Or tell about someone else's class reunion.
4. What kinds of feelings do people have when they get a divorce? How about when they get married? Or tell how people feel when they are in love.

Dialogue

Listen to the following dialogue with your books closed. Take notes as you listen, so you can ask your teacher any questions you may have.

CAST OF CHARACTERS

NASER	**FATIMA**
SAFFI	**FARRAH**
NINA	

(At a 10-year high school reunion being held in a restaurant)
Saffi, Farrah, and Nina are old girlfriends from high school. When they were in high school, they all liked the same guy, Naser. He liked them, but not as girlfriends. They were hurt by this. But that was a long time ago. Now, they are very excited to see him again.)

(Before entering the reunion)

Saffi: You guys, I'm a little nervous to see Naser. I wonder how he looks.

Farrah: I'm curious to see if he's married or not.

Nina: Oh, I hope not. How do I look? How's my hair? Is there lipstick on my teeth? Do you think my dress is fancy enough?

Saffi: Gees, Nina. You need to loosen up.

Farrah: It sounds like you still have feelings for Naser.

Saffi: Let's go. I'm anxious to see everybody.

(Inside the restaurant)

Farrah: Look at Mike. He has changed a lot. He kind of looks terrible. Don't you think so?

Saffi: Yeah. I heard he recently got divorced. He's probably feeling lonely these days.

Farrah: Oh, that's too bad. I'm going to go talk to him.

Saffi: Okay. Nina, how about getting a drink with me?

Nina: Okay. I guess so. Have you seen him yet?

Saffi: Seen who? Oh, Naser. Come on, Nina. Just relax, have fun. Don't worry about him.

(At the bar)

Nina: Look! There he is.

Saffi: Shhh! Don't yell.

Nina: I can't help it. I'm shaking like a leaf.

Saffi: Calm down. Take a deep breath and let's go say "Hi." Hi, Naser. How have you been?

Naser: Saffi, I'm fine. It's so good to see you. You look great. And, Nina, you look like a million bucks. What have you two been up to?

Nina: I just got a new job at Raleigh Computers as director of sales.

Naser: Good for you. I'm not surprised at all. I knew you'd do well. What about you, Saffi?

Saffi: I'm working in administration at State University.

Naser: Really? That sounds interesting. Let me get my drinks and I'll be right back.

(Farrah comes over to Saffi and Nina)

Farrah: Hey you guys, I've been talking to Mike. He's really depressed about his divorce, so I told him to call me the next time he feels down. By the way, you'll never guess who else I ran into — Fatima. She looks outstanding and seems real content with her life.

Saffi: I'm happy for her. Remember how quiet and studious she used to be?

Nina: Yeah. She was so different from us. We were so social and outgoing.

Farrah: Wait a minute. I'm confused. Fatima is dancing with Naser, I think.

Nina: No way! That's impossible. I didn't think they were friends in high school.

(After a few minutes, Naser and Fatima join Saffi, Nina, and Farrah)

Naser: I'd like you all to meet my wife, Fatima. She was in our class. Do you remember her?

Farrah: Yeah, she and I were just talking. I'm surprised you didn't tell me you were married before.

Saffi: Congratulations! I'm thrilled for you.

Nina: I . . . I don't know what to say. I'm shocked.

Comprehension

Answer the following questions without looking back at the dialogue. If necessary, listen to the dialogue again.

1. Why is Nina so concerned about her looks?
2. How does Mike look? How does he feel? Why?
3. Why does Nina look like a million bucks?
4. How does Naser feel about Nina? How do you know?
5. Which of the three old girlfriends do you think is the most outgoing? Why?
6. Were Saffi, Farrah, and Nina good friends with Fatima in high school? Why, or why not?
7. What surprising news does Naser tell the three women? What are their reactions? Why do they react this way?

Language Focus

Read and Study

A complete question using action verbs generally follows the pattern below.

(Wh-word) + (helping verb) + subject + main verb + (object)

1. _____		Do	+	you	+	remember	+	her?
2. _____		Don't	+	you	+	think	+	so?
3. How	+	do	+	I	+	look?		
4. _____		Have	+	you	+	seen	+	him yet?
5. How	+	have	+	you	+	been?		

Look at the following questions taken from the dialogue. Pay attention to the structure of the questions. Can you locate the subject and verb in each question?

Yes/No questions	**Information questions/Present tense**
Do you remember her?	Have you seen him yet?
Don't you think so?	How have you been?

Information questions/Present Perfect tense

How do I look?

Note: Incomplete questions are used only in informal spoken language.

Seen who? What about you, Saffi? Remember how quiet and studious she used to be?

Activity

Use the pattern above to make questions you would ask an old friend you haven't seen in a long time.

1. (A question about his/her job)

   ____

2. (A question about his/her family)

   ____

3. (A question about where s/he lives)

   ____

4. (Another question)

   ____

5. (Another question)

   ____

Vocabulary Activities

Vocabulary Activity 1 GOOD OR BAD FEELINGS

In pairs or small groups, look at the vocabulary list and put the words, idioms, and expressions into the following three categories:

Positive Feelings	Neutral Feelings	Negative Feelings
thrilled	*surprised*	*bitter*

Vocabulary Activity 2 IDIOM MATCH

Following are nine new idiomatic expressions from this chapter. Find one-word items that express feelings or emotions that are similar to these expressions.

1. pooped — *exhausted*
2. to be scared to death —
3. to be on cloud nine —
4. to feel like a million bucks —
5. to feel like someone ran over you with a truck —
6. to loosen up —
7. to be about to drop dead —
8. to be shaking like a leaf —
9. to be, or feel, down —

Vocabulary Activity 3 QUICK THINKING

1. Divide the class into groups of four or five students. Then divide each group into two teams, A and B.
2. Put a stack of cards with the vocabulary words on them between the two teams.
3. Team A picks a card and reads the word to team B. Team B has two minutes to give the definition and a sentence, using the word or expression. The team gets one point for each correct answer.
4. Reverse the roles. (The team that gets the most points wins the game.)

Speaking Activities

Speaking Activity 1 CREATIVE STORYTELLING

1. In groups of three or four students, you will be making up stories within a two-minute time limit.
2. Your teacher will give you the first line of the story.
3. One student in each group will continue the story with another sentence.
4. The next student adds another sentence to the story, and so on.
5. Try to continue the story without periods of silence between speakers.

Example:

Teacher: Joyce is so sad today.

Student A: Joyce lost her favorite pen.

Student B: Her grandmother gave her that pen.

Student C: It could write in three different colors.

(There is still a minute left, so the story goes back to student A.)

Student A: She is looking everywhere, but she can't find the pen.

Student B: Then, when she goes home, she sees her baby brother chewing on the pen.

(The two minutes are over.)

Speaking Activity 2 DEAR TABBY

CULTURAL NOTE: Many American newspapers include an advice column. People write to the columnist and ask for advice with their personal problems. Then the columnist's suggestions, or advice, are printed in the newspaper.

The following letters were written by people who have some personal problems.

1. In pairs or small groups, read each person's letter. Make sure everyone in the group understands the problem.
2. Discuss possible solutions to the problems. What advice would you give? There are probably several different suggestions you could offer for each problem.
3. After you have discussed a few different solutions, choose the best one and share it with the whole class.

Dear Tabby,

Every night when my husband gets home from work, he's in a real bad mood. I know he's exhausted from working hard all day, but he hardly says anything to me. I feel like he's ignoring me. What can I do?

The Lonely Mrs. in Albuquerque

Dear Tabby,

I have two daughters who fight non-stop. I know that the younger one (who is 12) is jealous of the older one (who is 16). She wants to do the same things as the 16-year-old. For example, my wife and I allow the older daughter to go to the movies with a group of her friends without a parent being there. But we don't allow our 12-year-old to do this. We have tried to explain it to her, but she just yells at the top of her lungs at us. What advice can you give?

A Disrespected Parent in Charlotte

Dear Tabby,

I've been dating this woman for one year. I really love her, and I want to marry her eventually. But she wants to get married SOON. It's all she talks about. She's driving me crazy. How can I deal with her impatience?

Frustrated in Seattle

Dear Tabby,

I work in a factory assembling cars. My coworker and I both applied for a promotion. I work very hard, and often put in overtime. I even do work on the weekends. My coworker, on the other hand, only does his eight hours a day. I feel I really deserve the promotion, but yesterday our boss announced that my coworker got it. I'm shocked and very upset about this decision. Is there something I can do to change this situation?

Bitter in New York City

Dear Tabby,

I'm usually a very energetic and talkative person. My best friend is quieter and calmer than I am. I feel we became so close because opposites attract. However, recently while I was telling her about my weekend plans, she suddenly told me I am self-centered. Then, she started crying and hung up the phone. I can't understand what I did wrong, and I don't want to lose my friend.

Regretful in Key West

Speaking Activity 3 ROLL THE DICE

Below is the game board for Roll the Dice. You can play the game with one, two, or three players. To play the game, you will need one die and a marker for each player. Decide who will go first. Then, that person can roll the die. The first player should move the marker the number of squares that corresponds to the number on the die. Follow the directions in the square. Continue the game by taking turns. The first player to get to the "winner" square wins the game.

BEGIN HERE

- Tell how you feel today. Why do you feel this way?
- What is something that irritates you?
- When was the last time you were on cloud nine?
- Lose a turn.
- How do you act when you are very angry?
- Has there been a time in your life in which you felt lonely or scared? What was the situation?
- Go back 3 spaces.
- How do you usually react when people lose their temper with you?
- Move forward 2 spaces.
- What are you grateful for?
- When your life gets stressful, what do you do to relax?
- Tell about a time when you were scared to death.
- Ask someone in your group when he or she last felt jealous.
- You are on a 5-hour flight. A baby next to you has been crying for the last two hours. What do you do?
- Lose a turn.
- Describe a terrible accident you have witnessed.
- Ask some people in your group about the last time they screamed at the top of their lungs.
- What do you do when you're sad or depressed?
- What was the last thing you were confused about?
- You are the winner. What does it feel like to win?

Speaking Activity 4 MOOD DIARY

Below are many words describing moods, feelings, and emotions. Circle at least three words that describe the different ways you have felt throughout the past week. Ask a partner yes/no or wh- questions to get information about situations that made him or her feel the various feelings.

bitter	calm	content	moody
nervous	lazy	energetic	cool
confused	shocked	cheerful	relaxed
anxious	lonely	depressed	loss of your temper
surprised	frustrated	pooped	

Why ____?

What ____?

When ____?

Where ____?

How ____?

Yes/No question ____?

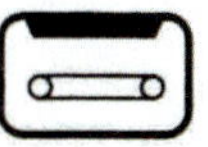

Listening Activities

Listening Activity 1 THE MANY MOODS OF ADAM'S DAY (A)

You will hear several conversations throughout one of Adam's days.

1. Read the questions for each conversation before you listen.
2. Listen to each short conversation and answer the corresponding questions.

Listening Activity 2 THE MANY MOODS OF ADAM'S DAY (B)

1. Listen to all the conversations together.
2. After listening the second time, chart Adam's moods for the whole day on a graph. Is this day similar to a typical day in your life? Explain.

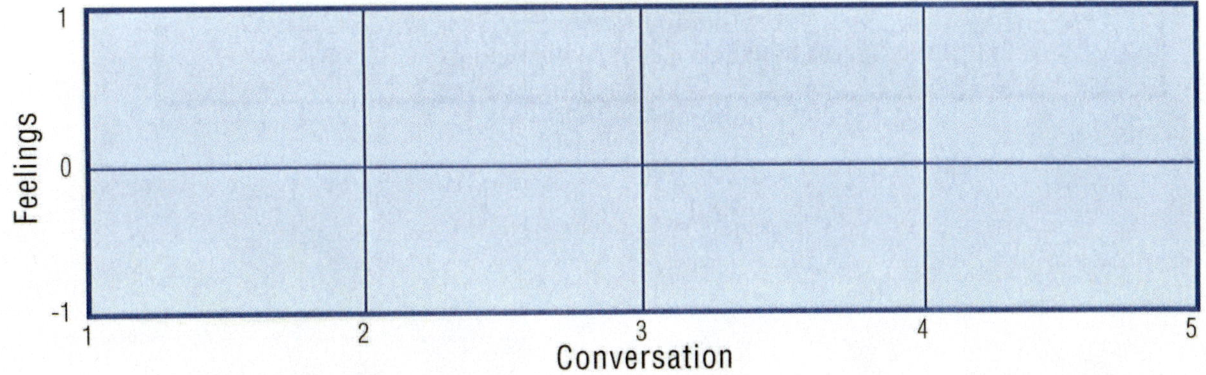

THE MANY MOODS OF ADAM'S DAY

Conversation 1

1. What do you think the relationship is between Adam and Ali?
2. Who is taking a test today?
3. How is Adam feeling this morning?

Conversation 2

1. Where are the speakers?
2. How did Adam do on his math test?
3. Why does Huda think she didn't do well on the test?
4. Why does Adam invite Huda to have lunch?

Conversation 3

1. Give two reasons why Adam doesn't like this class.
2. How did Nadia prepare for the test? What about Adam?

Conversation 4

1. What is Adam's job?
2. Why did the manager want to talk to Adam and Ahmed?
3. How is Adam feeling now?

Conversation 5

1. What is the relationship between Adam and Tarik? Why do you think so?
2. Why does Tarik call Adam?
3. How does Adam feel at the end of the conversation?

Crime, Law and the Judicial System

Brainstorming

Look at the picture below. Read and answer these questions:

What is the relationship between these people? Where are they? What are they watching? What do you think they are talking about?

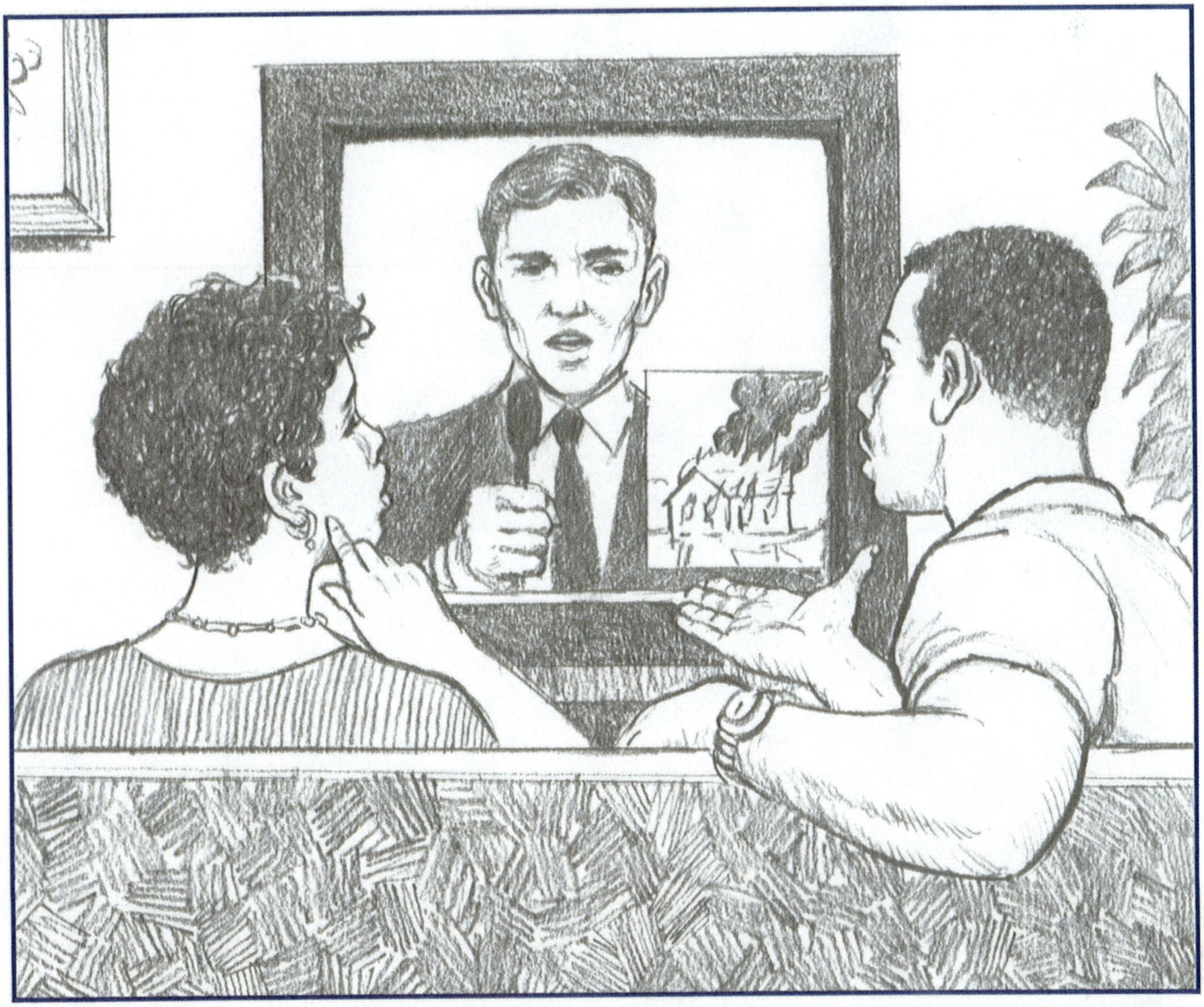

Vocabulary, Idioms, and Expressions

Practice pronouncing the following list of words and expressions. Then, take notes while your teacher gives the definitions.

Vocabulary (Crime)

gang
arson
to rob
rape
drive-by shooting
drug dealing/possession of drugs
DUI (driving under the influence)
to kidnap
burglary
to molest
suspect

Vocabulary (Judicial System and Law)

trial
jury
prosecution
defense attorney
to convict
prison
to arrest
investigator
innocent
court
defendant
prosecutor/prosecuting attorney
sentence
evidence
witness
victim
guilty
verdict

Vocabulary (Other Words)

jerk
obvious

Idioms and Expressions

to commit a crime
beyond a reasonable doubt
to get away with murder
freeze
to call to the stand
to be innocent until proven guilty
to be sick of something
under oath

Dialogue

Prelistening

Discuss the following questions.

1. How bad is crime in your country?
2. What are the most frequent crimes that occur in your country? What are the most frequent crimes that occur in the U.S.?
3. In your country, who decides if a person is guilty or innocent? Does your country have a jury system?
4. What rights does a suspect have in your country?

Dialogue

Listen to the following dialogue with your books closed. Take notes as you listen, so you can ask your teacher any questions you may have.

CAST OF CHARACTERS

SHERRY

TRENT

VOICE OF REPORTER

(A married couple is at home watching the news on TV.)

Sherry: I'm sick of watching the news. It's the same thing every time I turn it on: somebody was murdered, a store was robbed, three people were injured in a gang fight . . .

Trent: I know. I feel the same way. It seems like you can't trust anybody these days.

Voice of Reporter: Michael Harris was arrested today for murdering his wife and two children. He has also been charged with arson for burning down his own house.

Sherry: Can you believe that? This guy killed his own family. What a jerk!

Trent: Has the reporter given a reason for this crime?

Voice of Reporter: The couple had taken out a large life insurance policy, and investigators believe this could have led Harris to commit this awful crime.

Sherry: This is unbelievable. This man is so greedy.

Trent: Listen, he's explaining how it happened.

Voice of Reporter: The crime occurred when Harris was supposedly out of town on a business trip. All victims were sleeping when their house caught on fire. Apparently, they made no attempt to escape, because the remains of their bodies were found still in bed.

Sherry: Why didn't they wake up? This is weird.

(Note to the teacher: Stop the tape, and guess why they didn't wake up.)

(One month later, in Trent and Sherry's living room.)

Trent: What are you doing, sweetie?

Sherry: Shhh! They're talking about that Harris guy. His trial has started, and his doctor was interviewed and said that, one week before the murders, he wrote Harris a prescription for sleeping pills.

Trent: So, that's why they never woke up?

Voice of Reporter: Today in court, the prosecutor called a witness to the stand. This witness was a neighbor who says he saw Michael behind his house on the night of the murders and fire.

Sherry: It's so obvious that this guy did it. The pills and the witness are enough evidence for me. I'm sure the jury will convict him.

Trent: Yea, but he's innocent until proven guilty.

Sherry: He is guilty as far as I'm concerned.

Trent: Do you think the prosecution has proven his guilt beyond a reasonable doubt?

Voice of Reporter: The defense claims that it was dark on the night of the murders.

There is no way the neighbor could have seen Harris clearly. Besides, the hotel where the defendant was staying on his business trip has records of him checking in earlier that week.

Sherry: That doesn't prove anything. Where was he that night?

Voice of Reporter: However, the prosecution has found that Harris rented a car, and when he returned, there were rags covered in gasoline inside the car. In addition, the mileage on the car was high enough for him to have driven back to his hometown.

Trent: That's it. He's as guilty as sin. I hope the jury gives him a tough sentence.

(It's one week later, and the jury has reached a verdict.)

Trent: Sherry, come here. They are going to report on the verdict tonight.

Voice of Reporter: Today in court, Michael Harris was found not guilty for the murder of his wife and two children.

Sherry: What were the jury members thinking?

Trent: This guy actually got away with murder. In my opinion, our judicial system doesn't always do its job.

Comprehension

Answer the following questions without looking back at the dialogue. If necessary, listen to the dialogue again.

1. Why is Sherry sick of watching the news?
2. What crime is Michael Harris charged with?
3. Why does Sherry call Harris greedy?
4. How did the victims die?
5. Why is Sherry so sure that Harris is guilty?
6. How does the defense lawyer try to prove Harris' innocence?
7. Why were Sherry and Trent surprised by the verdict?

Language Focus

Read and Study

Sentence *intonation* is a very important aspect of spoken English. Recognizing and speaking with proper intonation is essential to communicating. This section will deal with *rising, falling*, and *even* intonation.

Affirmative and negative sentences

These sentences begin with even intonation, and then at the end of the sentence, there is a rising and falling pattern. This rising and falling pattern generally occurs when pronouncing a stressed word at the end of the sentence. Listen to your teacher pronounce these sentences from the dialogue.

I feel the same way.

This guy killed his own family.

This man is so greedy.

That doesn't prove anything.

Yes/No questions

Yes/No questions generally follow a rising pattern at the end of the sentences. Listen to your teacher pronounce these sentences from the dialogue.

Can you believe that?

Has the reporter given a reason for this crime?

Do you think the prosecution has proven his guilt beyond a reasonable doubt?

Information (Wh-) questions

Information questions beginning with *who, what, where, when, why,* or *how* generally follow the same intonation pattern heard in affirmative and negative sentences. Listen to your teacher pronounce these sentences from the dialogue.

Why didn't they wake up?

What are you doing, sweetie?

Where was he that night?

Choice questions

Choice questions use the conjunction *or* between the two parts of the question. There is rising intonation in the first part of the question, and falling intonation in the second part of the question. Listen to your teacher pronounce these sentences from the dialogue.

Would you like some coffee or tea?

Are you going shopping or to a movie?

Did the murderer use a gun or a knife?

Listing sentences

Sentences that list several words use rising intonation with each word in the list, except the final word, which has falling intonation. Listen to your teacher pronounce these sentences from the dialogue.

The detectives found gloves, blood stains, hair, and

clothing fiber at the scene of the crime.

You can get a ticket for driving too slow, too fast, recklessly, or under the influence.

Activity

With a partner, practice pronouncing and marking intonation patterns in the following sentences. (Partner A says the following sentences while Partner B marks the intonation.)

1. Do you know what time it is?
2. What would you like to have for lunch?
3. I would really like pesto pasta.
4. Will he be charged with murder in the first degree, in the second degree, or homicide?
5. Was he caught for drug dealing or using?

(Partner B says the following sentences while Partner A marks the intonation.)

1. Are we supposed to go north or south on the freeway?
2. There was a gang shoot-out last night.
3. Do you think he did it?
4. He has been convicted of burglary, kidnapping, rape, and murder.
5. Who shot the policeman?

Do you both agree on the intonation patterns? Check with your teacher to see if you are right.

Vocabulary Activities

Vocabulary Activity 1 WORD CLUES

1. Divide the class into two teams and decide which one will go first. Each team will be given one to two minutes for each turn of this activity.
2. One person from each team goes to the front of the classroom. The person from Team 1 is the player (speaker), and the person from Team 2 is the monitor.
3. The player picks a card from the teacher's stack. Do not show your card to anyone except the monitor.
4. The player describes the word, using complete sentences. (Do not use synonyms.) **Example:** Your word is *criminal.* You say: This is a person who does something wrong or illegal in society. (Do not use the synonym *culprit* to describe the word *criminal.*)
5. The goal is to get Team 1 to guess the word on the player's card. (Remember, the player is also on Team 1.) If the word is guessed and there is still time left, the player can pick another card.
6. While the player is speaking, the monitor has to listen for synonyms. If the monitor hears the player using a synonym, the player must stop speaking and Team 2 gets a point. However, if the player uses a synonym and the monitor doesn't hear it, the player can continue to describe the word.
7. The teams should switch roles until each person has been a player and a monitor at least one time.

Vocabulary Activity 2 SENTENCE HALVES

1. The teacher will give each person in the class half of a sentence.
2. Students who have the first half of the sentences line up in front of the class. Those with the second half of the sentences remain seated.
3. One at a time, the students who are standing read their half.
4. The seated students listen to see if their half completes the sentence being read.
5. If they think it does complete the sentence, they must read their half to the class.
6. The whole class then judges whether the two halves make one, whole, meaningful sentence.

Speaking Activities

Speaking Activity 1 NEWSWATCH

For this activity, you must watch the news for two days or nights at home, and then bring your listening logs to class for discussion.

1. Fill out the listening log below for the two times you watched the news.
2. Choose one crime to report about for each time you watched the news.
3. On the day of this activity, you will report on two crimes.

What crimes did the news present each day you listened? Check the appropriate boxes in the listening log.

Crimes	Day One	Day Two
gang violence		
murder		
mugging		
rape or other sexual crimes		
drive-by shooting		
drug dealing or possession of drugs		
kidnapping		
arson		
robbery		
burglary		
other		

Choose a crime for each day and fill in the following information. Circle yes or no.

Day One

What was the crime?____

Is there a suspect? yes no

Has someone been arrested? yes no

Describe the suspect or criminal. ______________________________

____

Was there a victim or victims? yes no

Describe the victim or victims. ________________________________

____

Has the trial begun? yes no

If yes, what is happening in the trial? ___________________________

____

Has there been a verdict? yes no

If yes, what was the verdict?___________________________________

If no, what do you think the verdict should be?____________________

____

Day Two

What was the crime? ____

Is there a suspect? yes no

Has someone been arrested? yes no

Describe the suspect or criminal. ______________________________

____

Was there a victim or victims? yes no

Describe the victim or victims. ________________________________

____

Has the trial begun? yes no

If yes, what is happening in the trial? ___________________________

____

Has there been a verdict? yes no

If yes, what was the verdict?___________________________________

If no, what do you think the verdict should be?____________________

____

Speaking Activity 2 MOCK TRIAL

A crime has been committed in your city. You and your classmates will act out the court trial for this crime.

1. Divide the class into groups. Members of each group will play one of the following roles:

    suspect
    defense attorney
    prosecutor
    judge
    victim (if the victim is alive)
    witness or witnesses
    police officer (optional)

2. With your group members, decide on the crime committed and which role each person will play in the court trial for this crime.
3. Prepare arguments for the defense and the prosecution of this case.
   Practice your trial, then perform it for the whole class.
4. The other groups serve as the jury and decide the verdict for the case.

Speaking Activity 3 NEW SOCIETY JUDICIAL SYSTEM

You and the other members of your group are victims of a shipwreck and have ended up on a deserted island. There is little possibility of rescue, so you must make up your own rules for a new society.

1. With your group, make decisions about the following:
    a. What actions will be considered crimes?
    b. Create a judicial system for your new society. In other words, who will decide whether a suspect is guilty or innocent, and how will that decision be made? (Be imaginative. Don't just copy a country's judicial system. Create your own unique system.)
    c. What punishments will be given for the crimes listed in "a" above?
2. Present your new society to the whole class.

Speaking Activity 4 CRIME PREVENTION

1. Discuss how you can prevent being a victim of crime.
2. Discuss how you can get help if you have been a victim of crime.

Speaking Activity 5 SPEECH

For this activity, you will prepare a speech to last three to four minutes. Choose from the following topics:

- Crime in your country compared to crime in the U.S.
- The judicial system in your country or in the U.S.
- Punishment or sentencing for various crimes.
- The death penalty and capital punishment.
- Crime prevention and safety.

1. You may prepare notes to look at occasionally while you speak. However, you should not read your notes. Try to speak as naturally as possible.
2. You can give your opinions on the topics, but you must support your opinions with examples or reasons.
3. The diagram below is a suggested way to organize your speech.

Introduction: Introduce the topic and main idea or ideas.
Body: Give examples or reasons supporting the main idea or ideas.
Conclusion: Closing comments.

Listening Activity

CLOSING ARGUMENTS

You will hear a prosecutor and a defense attorney give their closing arguments. Write the main points of each lawyer's argument in the chart below.

Prosecution Arguments	Defense Arguments

Listen to the arguments again if necessary. Then, check your answers. What do you think the verdict should be? What do the other members of your class think?

Holidays and Celebrations

Brainstorming

Look at the pictures below. Read and answer these questions:
What are the people doing in each picture? What is the relationship between the people?

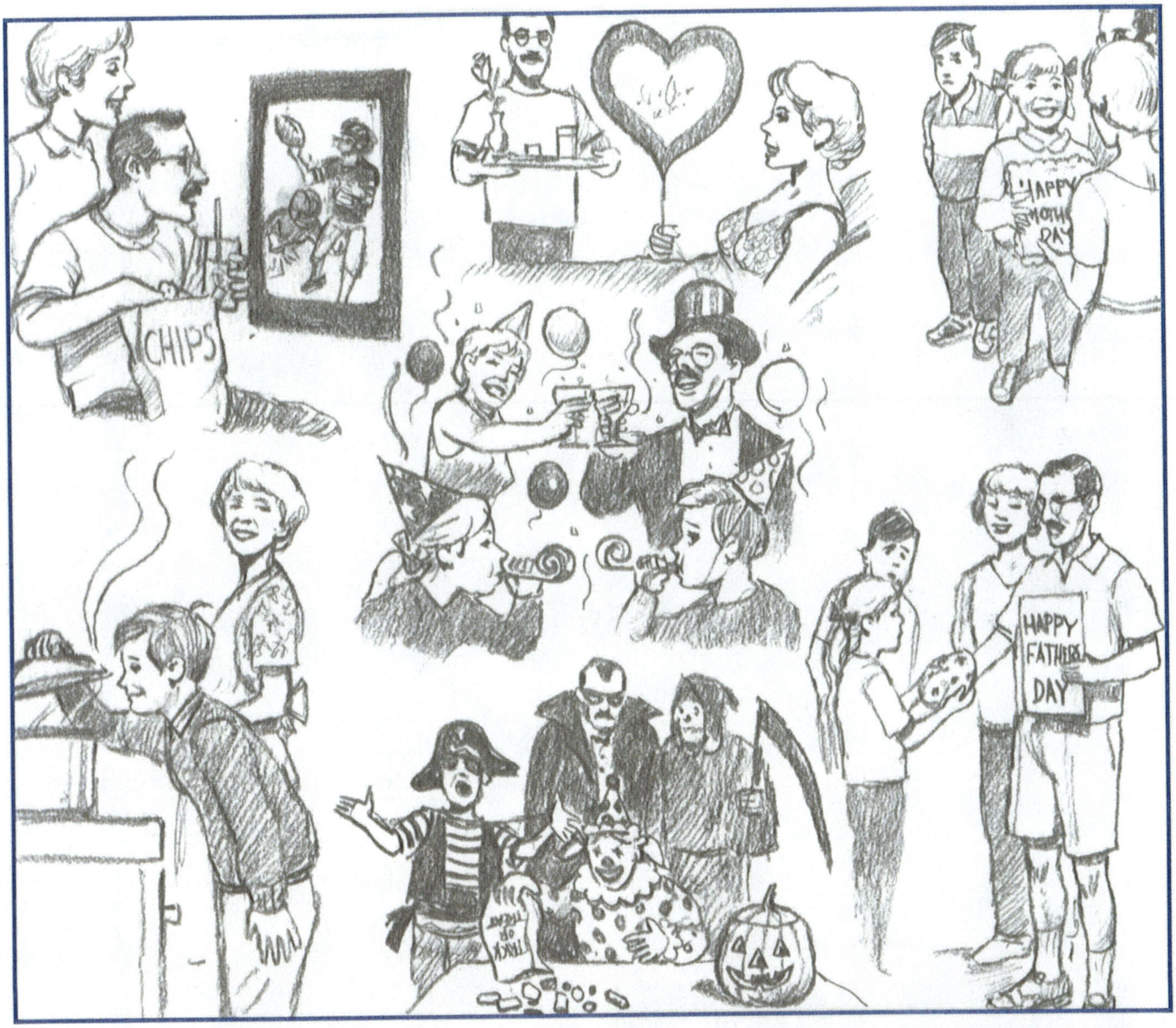

Vocabulary, Idioms, and Expressions

Practice pronouncing the following list of words and expressions. Then, take notes while your teacher gives the definitions.

Vocabulary

resolution
thoughtful
absolutely
thankful
feast
to tease
baby-sitter
sucker
eve
costume
tradition
to celebrate
attitude
to entertain
lollipop
decoration

Idioms and Expressions

out of the question
to kiss up to
to stand a chance
to kick butt
to take care of something
from now on
to make a toast
here's to...
Honey (Hon)
trick-or-treat
wimp

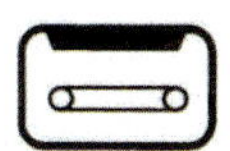

Dialogue

Prelistening

Fill in the chart below with the American holidays you know about, and then add any holidays from your country. Discuss these holidays.

Month	Holiday Name	Holiday Traditions: Food, Customs, Clothes	Type of Holiday: Religious, National, or Cultural
January			
February			
March			
April			
May			
June			
July			
August			
September			
October			
November			
December			

Dialogue

Listen to the following dialogue with your books closed. Take notes as you listen, so you can ask your teacher any questions you may have.

CAST OF CHARACTERS

LESLIE	**SARAH**
GARY	**DAVID**

(January 1st)

Leslie: I hope those 49ers win.

Gary: They don't stand a chance. The Cowboys are going to kick butt.

Leslie: Yeah, we'll see about that.

(February 14th)

Gary: Happy Valentine's day, Honey. I made breakfast in bed for you. Here you go.

Leslie: You are so sweet. You even brought me a flower. I love you.

Gary: And, don't forget, I'm taking you out to dinner tonight, too. So, please call the baby-sitter.

Leslie: Okay. I'll take care of it. Have a good day at work.

Gary: You too, Hon.

(Second Sunday in May)

Sarah: Happy Mother's day, Mommy. I made a card for you.

Leslie: Oh, thank you. It's beautiful.

Gary: David, didn't you get a card?

David: Oh, I forgot mine at school. But, I love you, Mom.

(Third Sunday in June)

Leslie: Happy Father's Day. You're a great father.

Gary: Thank you for the card. That was real thoughtful.

Sarah: Daddy, Daddy! Happy Father's Day. I made you a cookie. It's your favorite, chocolate chip.

David: Today is Father's Day? Oh, man. Hey, Dad, happy Father's Day.

(October 31st)

Sarah: Mom, Dad. . . look at all this candy.

Leslie: Don't eat any of that until I look at it.

David: Trick or treat, smell my feet, give me something good to eat. If you don't, I'll call the cops, and they will give me lollipops.

Gary: David, get that sucker out of your mouth and brush your teeth. The baby-sitter is here.

David: Where are you going?

Leslie: To a costume party.

Sarah: Your costumes are scary.

David: Don't be a wimp, Sarah. Hey, can we watch "Frankenstein" before bed?

Leslie: No, you have school in the morning. You can watch it tomorrow night.

David: That's not fair. I never get to stay up late.

(The fourth Thursday in November)

David: Mom, I'm hungry. It smells so good. Can I have my turkey now?

Leslie: No, your grandma and grandpa will be here soon. We're all eating together after they get here.

David: I don't want to eat with everybody else. I want to eat in front of the TV.

Leslie: That's absolutely out of the question.

David: Oh, man.

Gary: Sarah, what are you thankful for this year?

Sarah: To have such good parents.

David: Stop kissing up, Sarah.

(December 31st)

Gary: Let's make a toast to the new year.

Leslie: Here's to a great year. Well kids, what are your New Year's resolutions?

Sarah: I'm going to keep my room clean.

Gary: That'll be nice.

David: I think I'm going to change my attitude around the house.

Gary: You're kidding! How are you going to do that?

David: I'm going to do whatever you want me to from now on.

Leslie: Okay then, it's past your bedtime. You need to go to bed.

David: But Mom, you said I could stay up till midnight tonight.

Leslie: Ha, Ha. I'm just teasing.

Comprehension

Answer these questions without looking at the dialogue. If necessary, listen to it again.

1. What seven holidays are the family members celebrating?
2. What are Leslie and Gary doing on January 1st?
3. How are David's and Sarah's personalities different?
4. Why does Leslie ask the children not to eat their candy on October 31st?
5. Guess what kind of costumes the parents are wearing.
6. Why is it out of the question for David to eat in front of the TV on the fourth Thursday in November?
7. Why is David angry at Sarah?
8. What is Gary's reaction to David's resolution?
9. Do you think David will keep his resolution? Why or why not?

Language Focus

Read and Study

In English, some words are stressed and others are unstressed. The combination of these two produces sentence rhythm. Stressed words are slightly louder and spoken more clearly than unstressed words.

Listen to your teacher read these sentences from the dialogue. Can you hear the stressed syllables?

1. The cówboys are going to kíck bútt.
2. And don't forgét, I'm táking you out to dínner toníght.
3. But Móm, you sáid I could stáy up till midníght toníght.

Activity

Listen to the following sentences and mark the stressed syllables.

1. You even brought me a flower.
2. Have a good day at work.
3. Mom, Dad. . . look at all this candy.
4. Don't eat any of that until I look at it.
5. That's absolutely out of the question.

Vocabulary Activities

Vocabulary Activity 1 BINGO

1. Fill in the bingo card below with words from the vocabulary list on page 50. Put the words in any order. In other words, mix them up. Your card will be different from the other students' cards.
2. One student at a time will get a definition from the teacher. Read the definition to the class.
3. If the word being described is on your bingo card, put an X on that square.
4. If you are the first student to get five X's in a row (horizontally, vertically, or diagonally), you are the winner.

B	I	N	G	O

Vocabulary Activity 2 ASKING QUESTIONS

In groups of three or four students, ask questions, using the vocabulary words from this chapter. Take turns asking and answering the questions.

Example: If your word is *tradition*, you might ask, "What is a New Year's tradition in your country?"

Speaking Activities

Speaking Activity 1 FOUR NEW HOLIDAYS

1. Each student is given the name of an object.
2. Talk to your classmates to see if your objects are somehow related. If they are, you are in a group together. **Example:** If one student's object is a comb and the other student's object is a brush, then they are in the same group, because their objects are related.
3. As a group, plan a holiday celebration related to the objects. **Example:** If the objects are a brush and a comb, your group's holiday could be a celebration of hairstyles.

What is the holiday celebrating?
What will you eat during the celebration?
What will you wear?
What activities will occur in the celebration?
What decorations will you have?

4. Share your holiday celebrations with the class.

Speaking Activity 2(a) PICTURE DESCRIPTIONS

In pairs, take turns describing the pictures on this page and on the next page. One student will describe the pictures on this page, and the other student will describe the ones on the next page. Don't show your partner your pictures, and don't use the names of the holidays. Use at least four *complete* sentences to describe each picture. Guess which holiday your partner is describing. Student A describes the pictures below. Student B describes the pictures on the next page.

Speaking Activity 2(b) PICTURE QUESTIONS

1. In pairs, use the pictures from Speaking Activity 2(a).
2. One student looks at a picture.
3. The other student asks yes/no questions in order to guess which holiday is being celebrated in the picture. Again, don't use the name of the holiday in your questions.
   Example: Is there a pumpkin in your picture?
4. Reverse roles.

Speaking Activity 3 WHO DO YOU BELIEVE?

1. Individually, think of something interesting or unusual that has happened to you on a holiday. It can be exciting, scary, funny, sad, and so on.
2. Write one short sentence, describing this event. Don't give too much information in this sentence. **Example:** I burned my hand on the Fourth of July.

Your sentence: ____

____

3. Get together in small groups of three to five students. Share your sentences with the other members of your group. Then, write each member's sentence on a note card to be given to your teacher.
4. For homework, try to imagine all the details of the other students' incidents. You need to prepare a realistic story, with details for each sentence. (Where did it happen? Who were you with? How did it happen? What Happened next?) Don't write your ideas. Just think about them.

5. The next day in class, your teacher will choose one sentence from your group. You don't know which sentence will be chosen.
6. One at a time, each member of your group will describe the incident, including details. One person (the person who actually wrote the sentence) will be telling the truth. The other members of the group will be telling made-up stories. **Each group member's story will be different, because the imagined details will be different.**
7. After each person has told his or her story, the rest of the class votes for the one story they believed. Check with the presenting group to see if your vote was right or wrong.
8. The other groups will follow the same procedure.

Speaking Activity 4 PARTIES

Discuss the following:

1. How many of the parties listed below are you familiar with?
2. Discuss what happens at these parties.
3. What do people wear?
4. What do they eat?
5. If you don't know about a particular kind of party, guess what kind of party it is and share your ideas with the class.
6. If your guesses were incorrect, find out the correct information.
7. Talk about any additional parties that are not on the list below.

potluck	luau
progressive dinner	tailgate
toga	shower
Tupperware	sleepover
b.y.o.b.	50s
house-warming	bon voyage
happy hour	wedding reception
bachelor	costume
engagement	birthday
graduation	bar mitzvah
bas mitzvah	surprise
barbecue	Super Bowl
anniversary	beach
fraternity	sorority

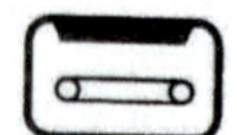

Listening Activities

Listening Activity 1 SHORT TAKES

Listen to the following short conversations, and then circle the correct statement about the conversations.

1. a. The boy doesn't want the girl to eat candy.
   b. The boy doesn't want the girl to eat his candy.
2. a. The boy doesn't want another hot dog, because he's full.
   b. The boy has already eaten a hot dog.
3. a. The man doesn't want to do anything special for the holiday.
   b. The man is looking forward to celebrating the holiday.
4. a. The woman did a lot of Christmas shopping this year.
   b. The woman will go shopping to save money.
5. a. The man usually takes this woman to nice places for her birthday.
   b. The woman has not been satisfied with past birthdays.

Listening Activity 2 THE FATHERS OF THE COUNTRY

Listen to the speaker talk about two great presidents.

1. What is the main idea of this lecture?

   ____

2. What was the speaker probably talking about before this passage?

   ____

3. What will she or he probably discuss next?
   a. more information about Washington
   b. more information about Lincoln
   c. the war between the North and the South

Write the numbers 1-5 next to the ideas listed below, in the order they are presented.

_____ They didn't have much schooling.

_____ He tried to keep the country united.

_____ He was a great first president.

_____ He became a lawyer, and later a politician.

_____ He helped abolish slavery.

Vacations and Travel

Brainstorming

Look at the picture below. Read and answer these questions:

Where are these people? What are they doing?

Where are they going? Are they having fun?

What is their relationship?

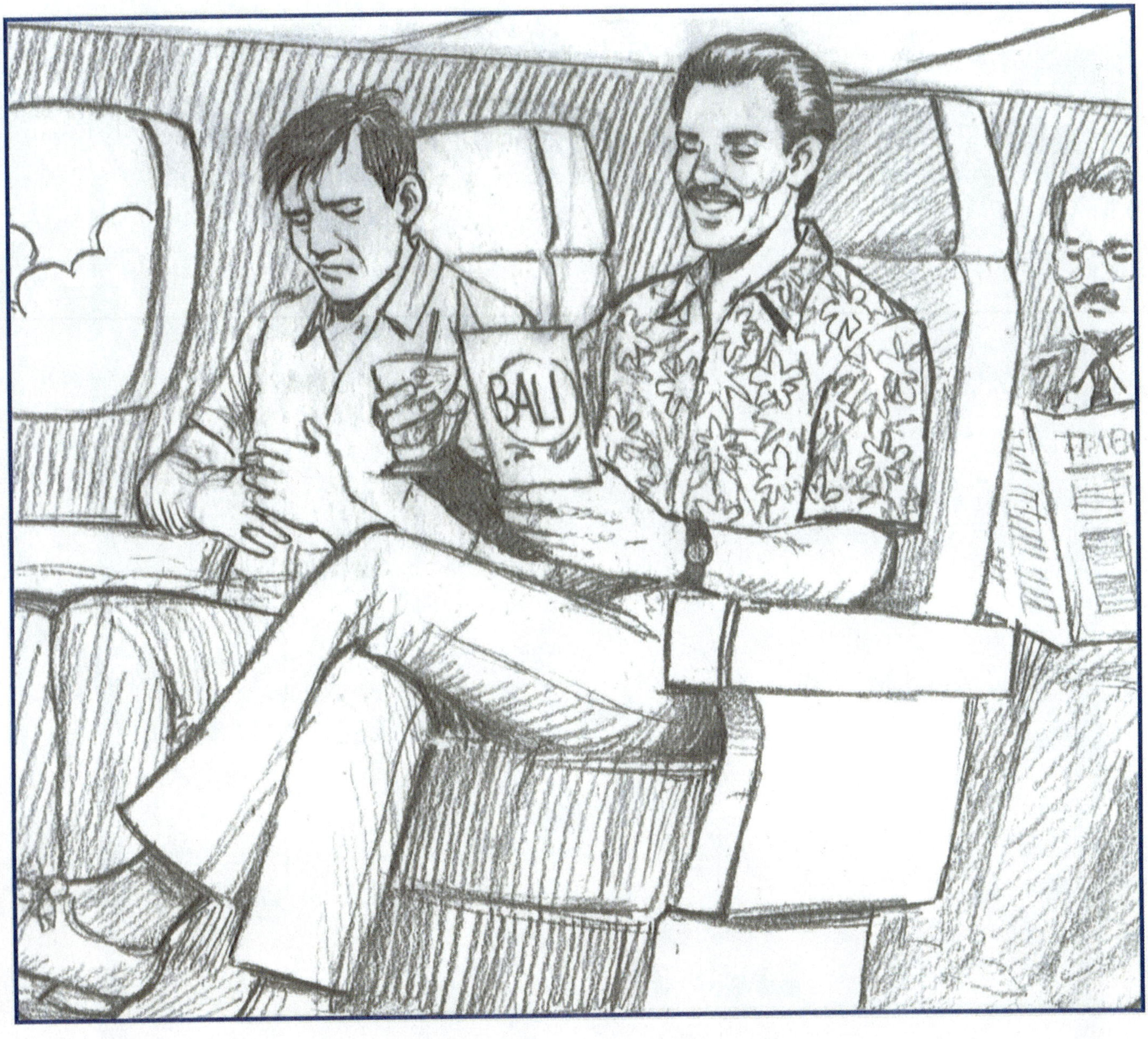

Vocabulary, Idioms, and Expressions

Practice pronouncing the following list of words and expressions. Then, take notes while your teacher gives the definitions.

Vocabulary (Airlines)

baggage claim
to depart
to fasten
destination
mileage
upgrade
to overbook
motion sickness
to check
reservation
to board
itinerary
gate
carry-on
standby
frequent flyer (program)
voucher
turbulence
ticket agent
to check in
skycap

Other Vocabulary

tourist attraction
volunteer
souvenir
tropical
brochure
to explore

Idioms and Expressions

top-of-the-line
have a blast
all expense paid
to be set
supposed to
to be in a rush
jet lag
frequent flyer (program)
pretty + adjective (pretty good, pretty nice)
What's up?
How about it?
to go for it
to get off to a good/bad start

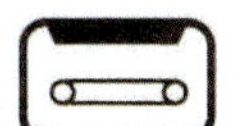

Dialogue

Prelistening

Discuss the following questions.

1. Do you like to travel by airplane? Why or why not?
2. Tell about what a passenger does in an airport before boarding a plane. What about after getting off the plane?
3. Have you had a bad travel experience on an airplane? If so, what happened? If not, ask someone else about their bad travel experiences.
4. Describe the best vacation you have ever taken.
5. What usually happens if an airline overbooks a flight?
6. If you have never traveled by plane, ask someone about their experiences. Then ask them the questions above.

Dialogue

Listen to the following dialogue with your books closed. Take notes as you listen, so you can ask your teacher any questions you may have.

CAST OF CHARACTERS

JOSE	**ROBERTO**
PILOT	**FLIGHT ATTENDANT**
TICKET AGENT	**VOICE ON LOUDSPEAKER**

(On the telephone)

Roberto: Hello.

José: Hey, Roberto. It's José. How's it going?

Roberto: Pretty good. What's up?

José: I have some good news. How would you like to go with me on an all expense paid vacation to Bali, Indonesia?

Roberto: What are you talking about? How can you afford that?

José: Well, I've been saving mileage on my frequent flyer plan for the last 10 years. And you know how much I travel for my job.

Roberto: This is unbelievable. You never told me about this before.

José: Well, how about it?

Roberto: José, you know I'd love to go to Bali. It's supposed to be the most beautiful tropical island on earth.

José: Okay, then. Mark your calendar for December 17th through the 24th.

(At the airport)

Ticket agent: Good morning. How many will be traveling today?

José: Two.

Ticket agent: How many bags are you checking?

Roberto: Just two. This one is a carry-on.

Ticket agent: All right, you are all set. Your plane will be departing from gate 10 in about one hour. Enjoy your flight.

José: Thanks.

(At the gate)

José: Look at all these people.

Roberto: Yea, it's the holiday season.

Voice on loudspeaker: Attention passengers on Flight 234 to Jakarta. Today's flight is overbooked. If any passengers wish to volunteer to standby, the airline will upgrade your tickets to first class for the afternoon flight. The airline will also give you a free travel voucher worth 400 dollars.

Roberto: Let's go for it, José. Let's travel in luxury.

José: Okay, I'm in no rush. I'm on vacation.

Roberto: This is going to be the best vacation of my life.

(On the plane)

José: Look at the hotel brochure. It's supposed to be one of the nicest ones on the island.

Roberto: Wow, look at the view. It's gorgeous. And there's even a bar in the swimming pool.

Flight attendant: Can I get you two gentlemen something to drink, and an appetizer before dinner?

Roberto: An appetizer! I love flying first class.

(About half an hour later)

Pilot: This is your pilot speaking. There's a typhoon heading toward Indonesia, and we are experiencing some turbulence. So please remain seated, with your seat belts fastened, until I turn off the "fasten seat belt" sign.

José: Oh no. I hate turbulence. I tend to get motion sickness. I don't feel so good.

Roberto: I have some motion sickness pills. Take one and you'll feel better.

(At the Jakarta International Airport baggage claim)

Roberto: José, you still don't look so good.

José: That medicine you gave me didn't work. I'll be right back.

(A few minutes later)

José: Have our bags come yet?

Roberto: No, and it looks like everyone else on our flight has left.

José: You're kidding! Our bags are lost?

Roberto: You know, they probably were on the morning plane.

José: Oh, great. This vacation isn't getting off to a good start.

(In a taxi, on the way to the hotel in Bali)

Roberto: We're almost there. You'll feel better once you get some rest.

José: I guess so.

(At the hotel)

Roberto: José, I thought you said this hotel was top-of-the-line.

José: This stinks. The weather is rotten, we have no luggage, our hotel is a pit, and I need to throw up again.

Roberto: Oh boy, some free vacation this is.

Comprehension

Answer the following questions without looking back at the dialogue. If necessary, listen to the dialogue again.

1. Why does José call Roberto?
2. Does José have enough money to take Roberto on a trip?
3. How can José take Roberto on an all expense paid vacation?
4. How many bags do José and Roberto have?
5. Why does the airline ask for people to volunteer to fly standby?
6. Why do José and Roberto want to volunteer to be standby passengers?
7. How does their flight begin?
8. What happens when the plane experiences turbulence?
9. After the plane lands, and José and Roberto are at the baggage claim, where does José go for a few minutes?
10. Why does Roberto say, "Some free vacation this is"?
11. What do you think the remainder of their vacation will be like?

Language Focus

Read and Study

There are several ways to express the future in English. Two common ways are:

1. be + going + to + base form of the verb
2. will + base form of the verb

These two forms are used in different situations.

Be + going + to + base form of the verb is used to discuss future plans or predictions.

This is going to be the best vacation of my life. (prediction)
I'm going to go to the beach this weekend. (plan)
What are you going to do tonight? (plan)

Will + base form of the verb is used to express promises, favors, requests, refusals, and predictions.

I'll be right back. (promise)

The weather will be great in Jakarta. (prediction)

Will you pay for my ticket? (request)

I will be happy to pay for you. (offer)

I won't be at work tomorrow. (refusal)

Activity

Give sentences for the following situations. Use be + going + to + base verb, or will + base verb.

1. The telephone is ringing, and your roommate is busy.

   You say: ______________________________

   ____

2. Refuse to eat something because it looks bad.

   You say: ______________________________

   ____

3. Ask someone to do you a favor. (request)

   You say: ______________________________

   ____

4. What are your plans for the weekend?

   You say: ______________________________

   ____

5. Your friend is sick. What can you do to help?

   You say: ______________________________

   ____

6. Make a promise to your teacher to do something.

   You say: ______________________________

   ____

Vocabulary Activities

Vocabulary Activity 1 MISSING WORDS

1. Listen to your teacher read a passage with some words missing.
2. As you listen, fill in the blanks with words from the list below. Write only the words, not everything your teacher says.
3. After listening, share your answers with your classmates. Your teacher will write the most popular answers in the class on the board.
4. Listen again. Were the most popular answers correct? If they were, continue with a new passage. If not, do the activity again until the most popular answers are correct.

blast	reservation	to check
brochure	skycap	top-of-the-line
in a rush	supposed to	tourist attraction
itinerary	ticket agent	tropical
motion sickness	to be set	

Vocabulary Activity 2 GUESSING GAME

1. You will be given a card with a question on one side and an answer on the other. Do not show your card to anyone in the class.

On one side of your card	**On the other side**
Where am I?	*Baggage Claim.*

2. Take turns going to the front of the class. Read the question on your card, and then act out the answer. **For the example above, act like you are looking for bags and looking at name tags. Maybe even act like you are picking up a suitcase from the carousel.** Use your imagination, and use facial expressions.
3. The students should ask yes/no questions until they find out the right answer.

Example: Are you looking for something? / Yes.
Are you looking for a person? / No.
Did you lose something?/No.
Are you in the airport? / Yes, but what part of the airport?
Are you in the baggage claim area? / Yes, that's the answer.

Speaking Activities

Speaking Activity 1 CLASSMATE INTERVIEW

Discuss the following questions with your classmates.

1. What places have you traveled to?
2. Which was your favorite place? Why?
3. Which was your least favorite place? Why?
4. Have you ever had any problems when you were traveling? If yes, what happened?
5. What other places would you like to visit in the future? Why?
6. What is the ideal way for you to travel (on a train, plane, with your family, alone)?

Speaking Activity 2 VACATION ADVERTISEMENTS

1. In small groups, you and your classmates will create a radio advertisement for either a real or fictitious city.
2. You may want to include the following: the city's name, its geography (oceans, lakes, mountains, deserts) and tourist attractions, and things to do there.
3. Give all of your group members a chance to speak.
4. Present your advertisement to the whole class.
5. Take a poll to see which cities your classmates prefer to visit.

Example:

Speaker 1: Come to Los Angeles. In Los Angeles, you can meet famous movie stars. You will also want to go sightseeing at Universal Studios. If you are lucky, maybe you will even meet a director and become a movie star.

Speaker 2: Don't pack too much, because you will want space in your suitcase for the new things you will buy on Rodeo Drive. You may even want to bring an empty suitcase, so you can fill it with souvenirs to take back home with you.

Speaker 3: Call Y and A Travel Agency and make your reservations today. Come to Los Angeles. The stars are waiting for you.

Speaking Activity 3 TELEPHONE FUN

For this assignment, you will call a few businesses to get travel information.

First Day

1. Your teacher will assign you to a group. Your group will be given one of the assignments listed below.
2. With your group, decide on what information you would like to find out. Then decide on three to five questions you can ask in order to get the information. It's important that each member of your group asks the same questions so that the next day, you can compare your answers.
3. Make sure each member of the group chooses a different business to call.
4. Make the calls at home.

Second Day

5. With the same group from the day before, compare your answers.
6. How were the businesses the same? How were they different?
7. Your group should report the most interesting similarity or difference to the rest of the class.
8. With the whole class, discuss any problems you had on the phone. Can you figure out a better way to communicate your ideas?

a. Call different rent-a-car agencies to find out the price of renting a medium-size vehicle for one day.

b. Call different airlines.

c. Call different hotels or motels in the same general area.

d. Call different travel agencies to get information about vacations to the same location.

e. Call different local transportation offices (train, subway, taxi, bus) to get information about public transportation.

Speaking Activity 4 COMPARING HOMETOWNS

1. You and your classmates will find differences and similarities among your hometowns.
2. Take turns using the topics below to make statements about your hometown. Then ask a question about that same topic.

Example:

Speaker 1: My hometown is very crowded. Is your hometown crowded?

Speaker 2: No. There are many farms in my hometown. Are there farms in your hometown?

Speaker 1: No.

Topics

countryside or city
number of people
shopping
public transportation
weather
things to do
things to see
geography
entertainment
restaurants
other topics

Speaking Activity 5 TRAVELING ROLE PLAYS

With your classmates, act out the following situations. Your conversations should last about three to four minutes.

1. You are on a long flight. You worked all day and are very tired. You need the time to rest. The person next to you keeps talking to you and asking you questions. You try to close your eyes, but the person keeps talking to you. **(two students)**
2. You are on a one-hour boat trip and you just ate dinner. You are beginning to feel very sick. One of the crew members notices that you don't look so good. He or she gives you some advice. **(two students)**
3. You and one of your friends are on a trip. You stop at a restaurant for a snack. When you come out, you realize you locked your keys inside the car. You ask someone for help. **(three students)**
4. You're on vacation, and you're lying by the pool at your hotel. You start a conversation with the person next to you and find out you have something in common. **(two students)**

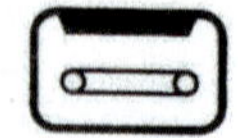

Listening Activities

Listening Activity 1 FOLLOW MARIA

María is visiting a new city. She has decided to go downtown and explore. Trace the path she takes through the city and put a dot (.) at each place she stops.

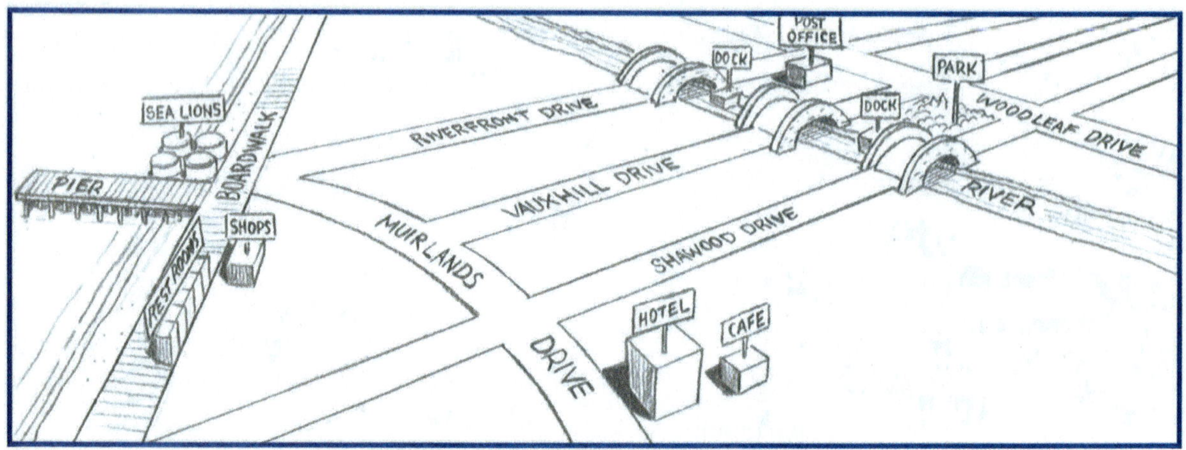

2. Listen, and then answer these questions.

a. Write **T** (true) or **F** (false) for the following statements.

_____ María crosses the Vauxhill Drive bridge.

_____ She mails her postcard at the corner of Shawood Drive and Woodleaf Drive.

_____ She crosses Riverfront Drive bridge.

b. Why does she wash her hands?

____

c. What information does the cashier give María?

____

Listening Activity 2 FIRST DAY ON THE JOB

Today is Enrique's first day as a flight attendant. He is nervous, and he makes a few mistakes on the airplane loudspeaker. Listen, and then write his five mistakes.

1. ______________________________
2. ______________________________
3. ______________________________
4. ______________________________
5. ______________________________

Movies and Entertainment

Brainstorming

Look at the picture below. Read and answer these questions:

Where are these people? What are they doing? What are they saying? What is their relationship?

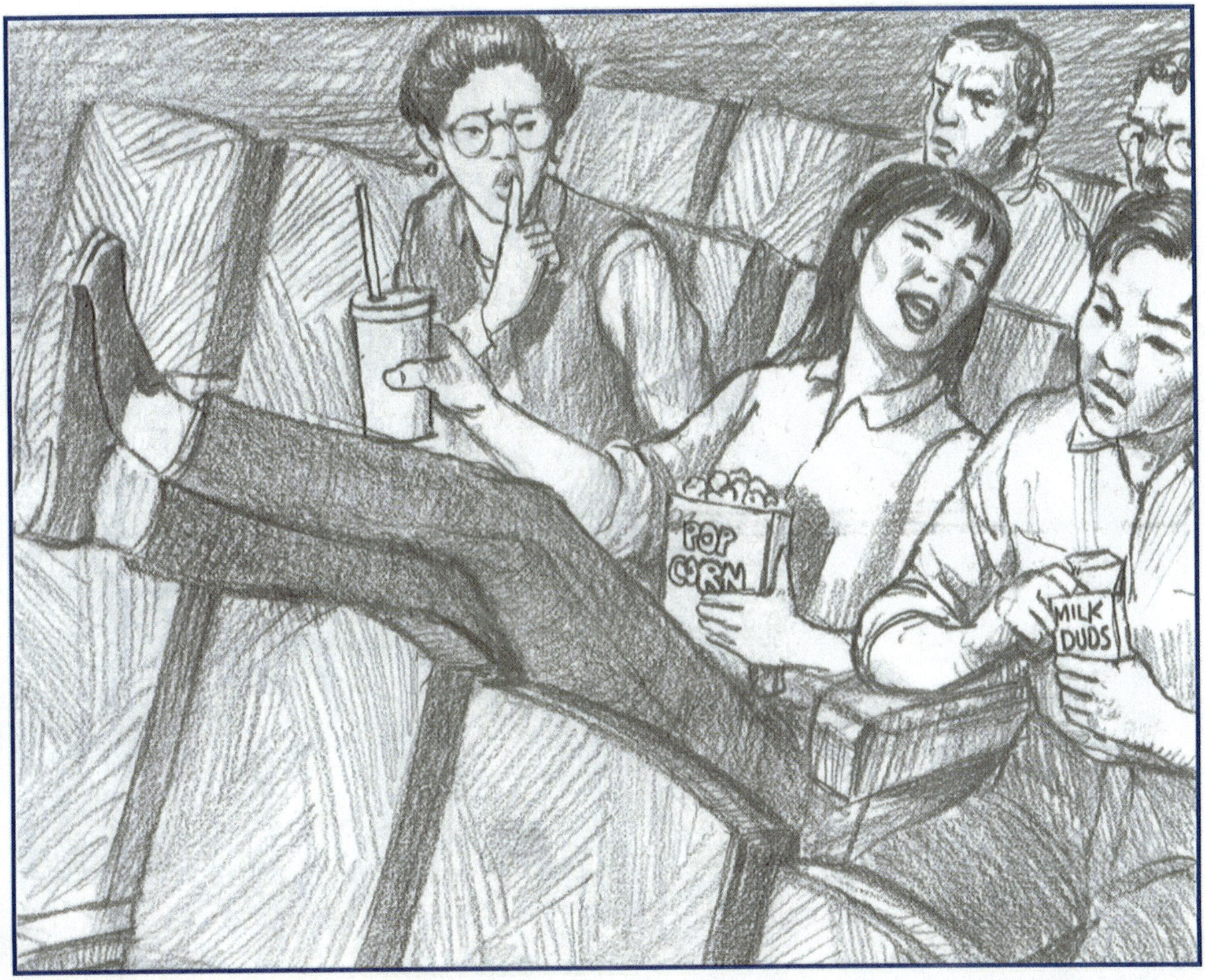

Vocabulary, Idioms, and Expressions

Practice pronouncing the following list of words and expressions. Then, take notes while your teacher gives the definitions.

Vocabulary

figure
record
salary
pile
file
stressed
sip
wig
to stare
drive-in movie
matinee
audience
to trigger
suspenseful
ratings
critic
movie review
to dim
performance

Idioms and Expressions

to kick back
to count on
sold out
to think straight
to run together
to play hooky
to lose one's mind
What do you say?
to get fired
to make up one's mind
to be out of here/there
to wait up
at a time like this
to live a little
flick

Dialogue

Prelistening

Discuss the following questions.

1. What do you do for entertainment?
2. What other forms of entertainment can you think of?
3. Tell about some different kinds of movies that you've seen.
4. What is the usual price of a movie ticket in the U.S.? How does that compare with the price in your country? Are there movie discount prices in your country?
5. What is considered proper etiquette in a movie theater in the U.S.?
6. Do employees' working habits change when their boss is not around?
7. Do people "play hooky" in your country?
8. Do coworkers ever socialize in your country? If yes, what do they do?

Dialogue

Listen to the following dialogue with your books closed. Take notes as you listen, so you can ask your teacher any questions you may have.

CAST OF CHARACTERS

VAN	**HUNG**
THUY	**BINH**

(In a business office)

Thuy: I'm so glad our boss isn't here today. I don't feel like working anymore. I'm just going to kick back this afternoon. In fact, I'm going to go call my boyfriend right now. If anyone calls, I'm not here.

Van: But we still need to take care of all the files over there. Binh is going to ask us about them tomorrow.

Thuy: They can wait.

Hung: We still have more files? It feels like we've already updated about a thousand.

Van: Come on, you guys. I can't do all this by myself. Binh is counting on us. Hung, could you read the figures to me and I'll record them in the computer.

Hung: Okay. I can't find their salaries.

Van: It would help if you were looking at the right files. Those are the ones we did this morning.

Hung: Van, my head hurts. I can't think straight. All these names and numbers are running together.

(Thuy comes back)

Thuy: Sounds like we need a break. I say we all play hooky for the rest of the day. Take a look at this newspaper. That new movie, "Life in the Fast Lane," is playing downtown.

Van: You've lost your mind, Thuy. Look at this pile of papers. There's no way we can leave this.

Thuy: What do you say, Hung? It's early enough to get the matinee price.

Hung: How much are matinees?

Thuy: They're half-price. Do you want to come or not?

Hung: Well, does that theater have Milk Duds?

Thuy: Of course.

Van: Are you guys serious? We might get fired for doing this.

Hung: Oh, I don't know what to do.

Thuy: Well, make up your mind. I'm out of here.

Hung: Okay, okay. I'm in the mood for Milk Duds. Let me get my glasses.

Van: I can't believe this. I don't want to stay in the office by myself. Wait up, I'm coming.

(In the theater)

Hung: These are the best Milk Duds I've ever tasted. Do you want some?

Van: No. I can't believe you can eat at a time like this. I'm so stressed. All I can think about are those papers on my desk.

Thuy: Hey, live a little. Have some popcorn, put your feet up, enjoy the flick.

Van: Thuy, you're not supposed to put your feet on the back of the chairs.

Thuy: So?

Hung: Could I have a sip of that? I've got some Milk Duds stuck in my teeth.

Thuy: Good, they're dimming the lights.

(A few minutes after the movie has begun)

Hung: Why is she wearing a wig?

Thuy: She doesn't want people to recognize her.

Hung: Why?

Thuy: In case there were any witnesses.

Hung: Oh.

Van: Be quiet! Everyone is staring at you two.

Hung: I'm sorry. I didn't realize we were disturbing the audience.

Thuy: (Makes a gasping noise.)

Hung: What? What happened?

Van: Shhh.

Thuy: She just triggered the alarm! They're going to find her now.

Hung: How did she trigger the alarm?

Thuy: Just watch the movie.

(After the movie, in the lobby)

Thuy: Wasn't that suspenseful?

Van: We better go back to the office now.

Thuy: Are you kidding?

Hung: Oh. Oh. Binh. Hi.

Comprehension

Answer the following questions without looking back at the dialogue. If necessary, listen to the dialogue again.

1. What is Thuy's attitude when Binh is not around?
2. Does Thuy leave the building when she says, "If anyone calls, I'm not here"?
3. Describe the three coworkers' personalities.
4. Why does Thuy say they need a break?
5. What finally convinces Hung to go to the movie?
6. Does Van enjoy the movie? Why or why not?
7. What do you think the movie is about?
8. How will this dialogue between Binh, Van, Hung, and Thuy continue?

Language Focus

Read and Study

Two commonly confused sounds in English are the **[th]** and **[s]** sounds, in which there is no vibration of the vocal cords. The **[th]** is made by placing the tip of your tongue loosely between your upper and lower teeth. Then, force air through your teeth around the tip of your tongue. Your lips should be relaxed. The **[s]** is made by placing your tongue in the middle of your mouth and pressing the sides of your tongue against the side of your upper teeth. Place your tongue forward, slightly touching the back of your upper teeth. Force air over the top of your tongue, making a hissing sound.

Listen to your teacher pronounce the following words, and repeat after him or her.

mouth	mouse
bath	bass
path	pass
think	sink

Language Focus Activity

This activity is done in pairs. One person circles one word from each pair below at random. Don't show your circled words to your partner. Then, say the word to your partner. Your partner should circle the words she or he hears. Then, switch roles.

Partner A		Partner B	
thank	sank	youth	use
myth	miss	forth	force
faith	face	thigh	sigh
thick	sick	math	mass
growth	gross	thin	sin
thing	sing	theme	seem
thumb	some	thought	sought

Vocabulary Activities

Vocabulary Activity 1 RELATED WORDS

1. Write varying forms of the vocabulary in the table below.
2. Complete the sentences below, using words from the table.
3. Finally, make your own sentences in your notebook, using the different forms.

Noun	Verb	Adjective
	to update	
pile		
	to record	
file		
sip		
		stressed
	to stare	
		suspenseful
rating		
critic		
	to dim	
performance		

1. The actress ____________________ very well in the movie.
2. After a while, his ____________________ began to bother her.
3. The child had low self-esteem because his parents were so ____________________ of him.
4. I always ____________________ when I have a big test.
5. She accidentally erased the ____________________, and he never got the message.
6. Don't ____________________ that tea yet. It's too hot.
7. He can create a romantic atmosphere in his house because he put ____________________ on all his lights.

8. I like ______________________ movies after I see them.
9. I just bought a new address book. I filled it in yesterday. Now, it's ______________________.
10. I'm thinking about going to that new restaurant. You have been there. How do you ______________________ it?
11. I need ______________________ my papers.
12. She enjoys the ______________________ of opening gifts.
13. He dances, sings, and acts. He's an all-around great ______________________.
14. My tape ______________________ needs new batteries.
15. Fold your clothes and ______________________ them on the bed. I'll put them away for you.
16. The ______________________ version of music is never as good as the live performance.
17. The room is so ______________________ that I can't read this book.

Vocabulary Activity 2 SPELLING CHALLENGE

1. Divide the class into pairs or small groups.
2. One person (person A) looks at the vocabulary list on page 74.
3. Person A chooses a word or expression, and writes blanks for the number of letters in that word or expression.

   Example: realize (7 letters) ___ ___ ___ ___ ___ ___ ___
4. The other person or persons (B,C, and so on) choose(s) five consonants and three vowels from the alphabet.
5. Person A fills in the letters that fit into the blanks. **Example:** Person B chooses c, l, t, s, b, and u, e, o. Person A fills in the blanks: ___ _e_ ___ _l_ ___ ___ _e_
6. Next, person B guesses what the word is.
7. If person B guesses the word, he or she makes a sentence with the word.
8. Then A and B switch roles.

Speaking Activities

Speaking Activity 1 TELEVISION AWARDS

This activity takes place over the course of two class meetings. Students will be the judges for TV awards.

1. The teacher brings a current TV listing to the class.
2. As a class, decide on two programs that everyone will watch that evening for homework.
3. Go home and watch the programs you have chosen. As you watch them, fill out the ballot below.

Best actor: ______________________________

Best costume: ______________________________

Best director: ______________________________

Best story line: ______________________________

Best set: ______________________________

4. During the next class meeting, form small groups.
5. Discuss your answers. Why did you make your choices?
6. If you had different answers, try to convince the other members of your group to change their minds.
7. After discussing all five categories, take a class vote to determine the winner for each category.

Speaking Activity 2 MOVIE CRITIQUE

In order to prepare for this activity, students will use in-class time as well as time at home.

1. Students form pairs and choose a movie on video to review.
2. Watch the movie at home with your partner.
3. As you watch it, critique, or evaluate, different aspects of the movie — the actors, music, costumes, story line, special effects, and setting.
4. Decide whether these aspects make the movie strong or weak. In other words, form an opinion about the movie.
5. It's OK for you and your partner to disagree.
6. Next, you and your partner prepare a critique of the movie and present it in class. You may use the outline on the next page as a guide.

Introduction: Introduce the film. What is it called? What type of movie is it? Give some background information about the story and characters. You can also introduce the actors.

Evaluation: Evaluate the different aspects of the movie. Remember, you and your partner don't have to agree.

Clip presentation: Show a scene from the movie that supports your evaluation. Your partner may show a different clip or use the same one.

Conclusion: Give your overall impression of the movie. Do you recommend it to the rest of the class? Why or why not?

The following vocabulary words may be useful in your critiques:

realistic	tear-jerker	thrilling
original	a waste of time	hilarious
extraordinary	sappy	bizarre

Speaking Activity 3 MUSIC LYRICS

1. Individually or with a partner, choose a song with lyrics sung in English.
2. Listen to the song at home and write down the lyrics as you hear them. If you can't understand some of the lyrics, leave a blank space.
3. The next day, bring the tape or CD to class.
4. Photocopy and pass out the lyrics you wrote the night before.
5. Play the song for the class. Encourage everybody to sing along with the song.
6. Explain why you chose this particular song. Why do you like it? How do you feel when you hear this song? When was the first time you heard it?

Speaking Activity 4 COMEDY SHOW

This activity involves telling jokes. If you don't know any, you must ask people to tell you jokes outside the class prior to this activity.

1. Share a joke that you have heard with a group of students.
2. Choose the funniest joke from your group to tell the whole class.
3. Choose jokes that are not offensive to any particular group of people.

Speaking Activity 5 GAMES

The games you teach in this activity can be card games, board games, or any other game that can be played in the classroom.

1. Choose a game, preferably from your country, to teach the class.
2. Teach the class how to play, either by explanation or demonstration.
3. Play the game.

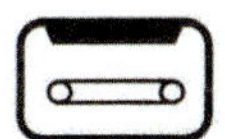

Listening Activities

Listening Activity 1 PICTURE PUZZLE

1. **Listen to the story, and then put the pictures in the correct order.**
2. **With a partner, retell the story. Do you two agree on the order of the pictures? Explain.**

Listening Activity 2 TELEPHONE MESSAGES

1. Phong comes home from work and finds four messages on his answering machine.
2. Listen to each message and take notes on the message pads below.

To: ______________________

______________________ called

at __________ A.M./P.M. on ________

Phone No. ______________________

Message: ______________________

____

____

____

____

____

To: ______________________

______________________ called

at __________ A.M./P.M. on ________

Phone No. ______________________

Message: ______________________

____

____

____

____

____

To: ______________________

______________________ called

at __________ A.M./P.M. on ________

Phone No. ______________________

Message: ______________________

____

____

____

____

____

To: ______________________

______________________ called

at __________ A.M./P.M. on ________

Phone No. ______________________

Message: ______________________

____

____

____

____

____

3. Which offer do you think Phong will accept?

Family and Lifestyles

Brainstorming

Look at the picture below. Read and answer these questions:

Where are these people? What are they doing? What are they talking about? What is their relationship to each other?

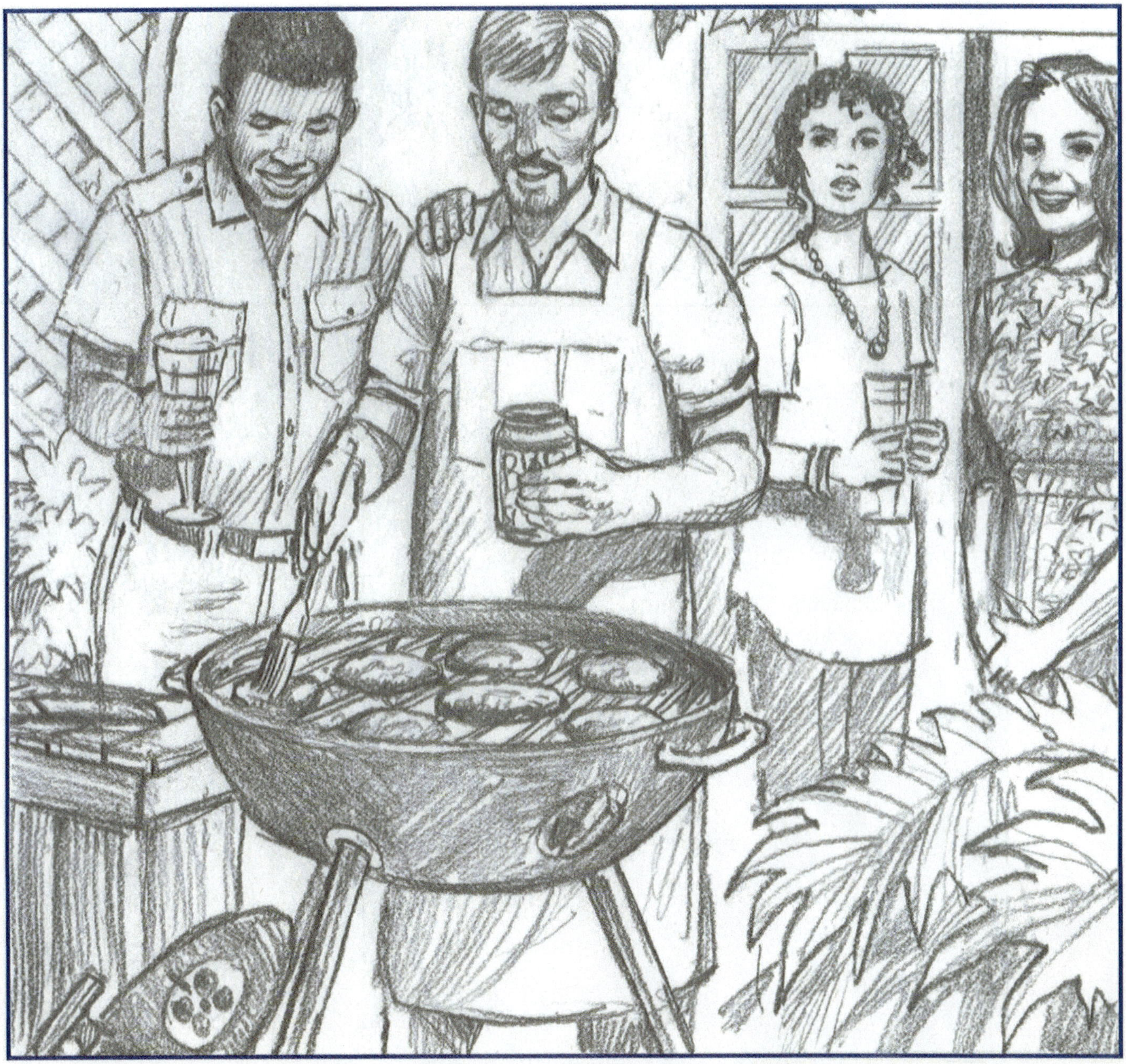

Vocabulary, Idioms, and Expressions

Practice pronouncing the following list of words and expressions. Then, take notes while your teacher gives the definitions.

Vocabulary

doorbell
refreshed
incredible
single-parent family
nuclear family
extended family
interior decorator
lifestyle
envy
alimony
generation
rejected
stress

Idioms and Expressions

to remember the last time you did something
to glow
to run late
What's new?
to never cease to amaze someone
to throw a temper tantrum
burn out
What I wouldn't do for . . . (something)
to have it made
to deal with
to expect less or more from someone
to pack up
to make out
to get the door

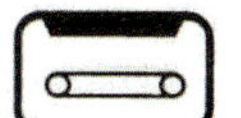

Dialogue

Prelistening

Discuss the following questions.

1. Who are the members of a nuclear family? What are their lifestyles usually like?
2. What are some other family structures? (A couple without children, for example.) How do their lifestyles differ?
3. What are the advantages and disadvantages of different family structures?
4. What are some problems that parents have with their children? How about with teenagers?

Dialogue

Listen to the following dialogue with your books closed. Take notes as you listen, so you can ask your teacher any questions you may have.

CAST OF CHARACTERS

GEORGE	**KATHY**
MATHIAN	**CINDY**

(Old friends are having a barbecue together at one of their houses. The doorbell has just rung.)

Kathy: Hi! How are you? Oh, you brought some beer. Great.

George: You look good. Have you gotten a haircut or something?

Kathy: No.

George: Well, there's something different about you.

Kathy: I just got back from a trip to Costa Rica. I probably got a little tan. And, let me tell you, I feel so refreshed. I didn't even think about work for one minute while I was there.

George: You're so lucky that you are single with no children. You can just pack up and leave at anytime.

Kathy: It's not exactly like that.

George: Well, you certainly are glowing. I can't remember the last time I had a vacation.

Kathy: George, you should take a vacation. You're going to burn out if you don't.

George: I know, but the alimony is killing me. I can't afford to take time off. Aren't Mathian and Cindy here yet?

Kathy: They just called. Their baby-sitter is running a little late. Let me put that in the refrigerator. Go on out back. I'll be there in a sec.

(In the backyard)

Kathy: So, what's new in your life?

George: Well, John never ceases to amaze me. Last night, I had to work late, so I didn't get home until about 9 o'clock. When I walked through the door, he was making out with his girlfriend.

Kathy: No way. Is he old enough to be doing that? Life with him must be pretty exciting.

(Doorbell rings)

Kathy: There they are. George, would you mind putting the chicken on the grill while I get the door?

(At the door)

Cindy: I'm sorry, Kathy. The baby-sitter was late. Then, Mark and Michelle had a huge fight. Mark wouldn't stop crying, and then when we started to leave, he threw a temper tantrum. Do you have any aspirin?

Kathy: Yes, I'll go get it for you. How can those two adorable kids give you a headache? They're so cute. You guys go on out into the back. George just started the chicken.

(In the backyard)

Mathian: What smells so good?

George: It's this chicken. Come here and taste this sauce Kathy made. It's incredible.

Mathian: Mmmm! Cindy, we'd better get this recipe. Kathy is the best cook I know.

Cindy: Yea, well, she has a little bit more time than some people. What I wouldn't do for a life like Kathy's.

George: Yea, she has it made.

Mathian: She's so lucky to have a hobby for a job.

Cindy: I wouldn't call it a hobby. She's the highest paid interior decorator in this city.

George: All I know is, she doesn't have to deal with teenagers.

Mathian: Or children.

(Kathy returns)

Kathy: Cindy, here's the aspirin you wanted. And, have some of this beer that George brought.

Mathian: Okay. Do you want me to open up one for you, Kathy?

Kathy: No, thanks.

George: But I got your favorite kind.

Kathy: I know. Would you come sit down. Everything is ready.

Cindy: Look at that salad.

Kathy: All the vegetables came from the garden.

Mathian: Of course! We wouldn't expect less from you.

Kathy: Ha ha. Well, I invited you all to tell you news.

Cindy: What? Did you meet a man?

Kathy: Not exactly. I don't know how to say this, umm... I'm having a baby.

Comprehension

Answer the following questions without looking back at the dialogue. If necessary, listen to the dialogue again.

1. Is it easy for George to take a vacation? Give reasons.
2. Who is John? How old do you think he is?
3. Who are Mark and Michelle? How old do you think they are?
4. Why does Cindy ask for aspirin?
5. Why does Cindy envy Kathy?
6. Why does George envy Kathy?
7. Why does Mathian envy Kathy?
8. Does Kathy envy the others? How do you know?
9. Why doesn't Kathy accept her favorite beer?
10. How do you think Kathy feels about the news she shares with her friends?
11. Describe Kathy's home and lifestyle now. Do you think they will change? If so, how?
12. How might Kathy's friends react to her news? Why?

Language Focus

Read and Study

The past tense is used to discuss actions or situations that started in the past and are now finished.

Examples: things that occurred yesterday, last week, two hours ago, in 1996.

They rent<u>ed</u> an apartment yesterday. I call<u>ed</u> her last week.

She walk<u>ed</u> to school two hours ago. They play<u>ed</u> professional baseball in 1996.

Most past tense verbs in affirmative sentences are formed by adding **-ed** to the simple base form of the verb. There are also several irregular past tense verbs for affirmative sentences (see Appendix II). Look at the following affirmative past tense sentences taken from the dialogue.

Affirmative Past Tense

subject	+	(adverb)	+	past tense verb (-ed or irregular form)	+	object.
1. I	+	probably	+	got	+	a little tan.
2. I	+	———	+	was	+	there.
3. I	+	———	+	walked	+	through the door.
4. George	+	just	+	started + the chicken.		

Past tense negative sentences are formed by using didn't + the simple base form of the verb.

Negative Past Tense

subject	+	didn't	+	simple base form of the verb	+	object.
1. I	+	didn't	+	think	+	about work for one minute.
2. I	+	didn't	+	get	+	home until 9 o'clock.

Language Focus Activity 1

Correct the mistakes in the past tense sentences below.

1. Jane's brother quitted his job last week.
2. I didn't went to the store yesterday.
3. I come to work late this morning.
4. He was run five miles yesterday.
5. Yvonne didn't talked to her boyfriend last night.

Language Focus Activity 2

Talk about a memorable time you had with your family (like a vacation, holiday, wedding, or family reunion). Pay attention to your use of the past tense.

Vocabulary Activities

Vocabulary Activity 1 SENTENCE SUBSTITUTION

1. Divide the class into two sides, A and B.
2. Side A looks at the sentences below, and side B looks at the vocabulary list on Page 86.
3. Side A reads the sentences one at a time. Side B restates each sentence, substituting some words with a vocabulary word or expression.
4. If the class agrees that the restated sentence has the same meaning as the first sentence, then the person who restated correctly can switch roles with the reader from side A.

Example: Side A students says, "Wait a minute. I have to tie my shoelace." Side B student restates the sentence by saying, "Wait a sec. I have to tie my shoelace."

Sentences to be read by side A

1. The little boy was shouting, crying, and kicking his feet because his Mom wouldn't buy him a new toy truck.
2. Eric's life is perfect because he has a great job and a loving family.
3. Juan can't handle his boss anymore, so he wants to quit his job.
4. I would do anything to have a baby.
5. Some people don't like to kiss for a long time on a first date.
6. It's unbelievable that Fatima has five sisters and nine brothers.
7. I've been working such long, hard hours. I'm so tired of working.
8. I'm really behind schedule today.
9. How's life?
10. After my shower, I feel like a new person.

Vocabulary Activity 2 VOCABULARY QUESTIONS

Ask your classmates the following questions.

1. Can you remember the last time you made out with someone?
2. Who was the last person who rang your doorbell?
3. What type of family structure did you grow up in?
4. Have you been in a house decorated by an interior decorator? If so, describe it. If not, ask someone who has been in a decorated house to tell you about it.
5. Do all pregnant women glow?
6. In your opinion, what is a good lifestyle?
7. What is something that never ceases to amaze you?

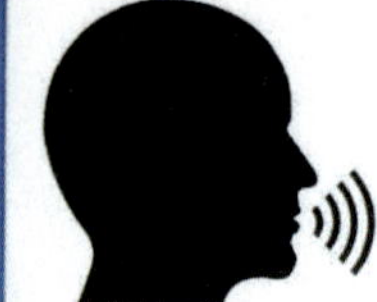

Speaking Activities

Speaking Activity 1 DESCRIBING LIFESTYLES

Look at the pictures of people below, and answer the questions about their lifestyles. Use your imagination to guess all aspects of their lifestyles.

Questions

1. What is each person in the pictures doing?
2. What is a typical day in each person's life like (food, stress, work, fun, sleep, exercise, material wealth)?
3. What do they do for a living?
4. What do they do in their free time?
5. Who do you think they live with?
6. What's their marital status?
7. What other guesses can you make about their lifestyles?

Speaking Activity 2 GENERATION COMPARISON

Fill in the table below with comparisons of the aspects of different lifestyles. How does your lifestyle differ from that of your grandparents and parents? How do you think your children's (or future generations') lifestyles will differ from yours? Look at the examples.

	Grandparents' Generation	Parents' Generation	Your Generation	Future Generations
Family Structure	*extended family, many children*	*nuclear family more divorces*	*nuclear family, single-parent families, more single people, fewer children*	*possibly less divorce, 0 or 1 child, etc.*
Male and Female Roles				
Responsibility				
Work				
Stress				
Exercise				
Free Time, Hobbies				
Food				
Travel/ Vacations				
Material Wealth				
Other				

Speaking Activity 3 LIFESTYLE OPINIONS

Choose one of the statements below. Then, ask each classmate his or her opinion of the statement. Take short notes and report the results to the whole class after you have talked to everyone.

1. A married couple shouldn't get divorced under any circumstances.
2. A couple should not live together unless they are married.
3. Adult children have a responsibility to take care of their elderly parents.
4. Homosexuals should have the right to marry.
5. Women should not work if they have young children.
6. It is acceptable for unmarried women to have children.
7. Wealthy people should give to the poor or disadvantaged.
8. Fourteen-year-olds are not old enough to go out on a date without supervision.
9. Parents should not leave their children with a baby-sitter for longer than one night.
10. A baby-sitter should be at least 12 years old.
11. Husbands should make more money than their wives.
12. Men should help with household chores around the house.
13. A man should make the rules for his family and home.
14. Parents should financially support their children until they find a job and/or get married.
15. People should not work more than 40 hours a week.
16. Husbands and wives should have some time every week to spend away from their families.
17. Pets should not be allowed inside people's homes.
18. Revealing clothes are tasteless.
19. If parents can afford it, their children should be given everything they want.
20. Parents should pay for their children's college education.
21. A couple's age should not differ by more than 12 years.
22. Teenagers should not be allowed to work during the school year.
23. Single people should look for a husband or wife.
24. A woman should not have children after she is 40 years old.
25. It's acceptable for a man to have children until he is 60 years old.
26. It is acceptable to drive after having only one alcoholic drink.
27. A couple should not marry unless they have the same religious background.
28. People should spend as much time on their hobbies as they do on their jobs.
29. People shouldn't buy items with credit cards.
30. Companies should give employees three weeks of vacation every year.

Speaking Activity 4 FAMILY DIFFERENCES

In groups of three or four students, discuss the following questions. Try to work with classmates who come from a background that is different from yours.

Student's First Name	1.	2.	3.	4.
Who did you live with while growing up?				
If you have siblings, what is your relationship with them like?				
Are you closer to your mother or your father?				
Who spent the most time raising you?				
Do you have a relationship with your grandparents? What is it like?				
How close are you with other relatives?				
Were you spoiled as a child? Explain?				
Were your parents strict?				
Did you vacation with your family? Where?				
Did you work while living with your family?				
Did you have a lot of responsibility as a child? Explain.				

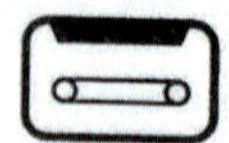

Listening Activities

Listening Activity 1(a)

Listen to the first part of a dialogue taken from part of a talk show about lifestyles. Fill in the blanks with the missing words.

Host: So, Leah, your parents were divorced, and you were raised by your father?

Leah: That's right.

Host: ____________ old were you when ____________ parents divorced?

Leah: I was 10.

Host: So, how ____________ you come to live with your father?

Leah: ____________ mother didn't have a job and really ____________ afford to take care of me, so my ____________ and I moved to a new place.

Host: How ____________ you think the divorce has affected you?

Leah: ____________ at first I felt like my mother ____________ love or want me. Living with my father ____________ fine, but I felt rejected by my mother. I wanted my parents to get ____________ together more than anything in the world.

Host: ____________ now?

Leah: I feel that I lost a lot ____________ my childhood because I was always worried ____________ my parents and whether they would ever ____________ back together. Of course, it still ____________ me, because I'm too scared to ____________ to anyone now.

Listening Activity 1(b) LIFESTYLES UP CLOSE

Listen to the whole dialogue from the talk show, and answer the questions.

1. ____________
2. ____________
3. ____________
4. ____________
5. ____________
6. ____________
7. ____________
8. ____________

Values and Beliefs

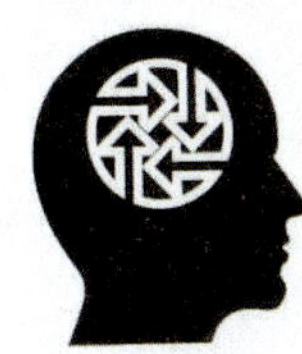

Brainstorming

Look at the picture below. Read and answer these questions:

Where are these people? What are they doing? What is their relationship to each other? What are they talking about? How old are they?

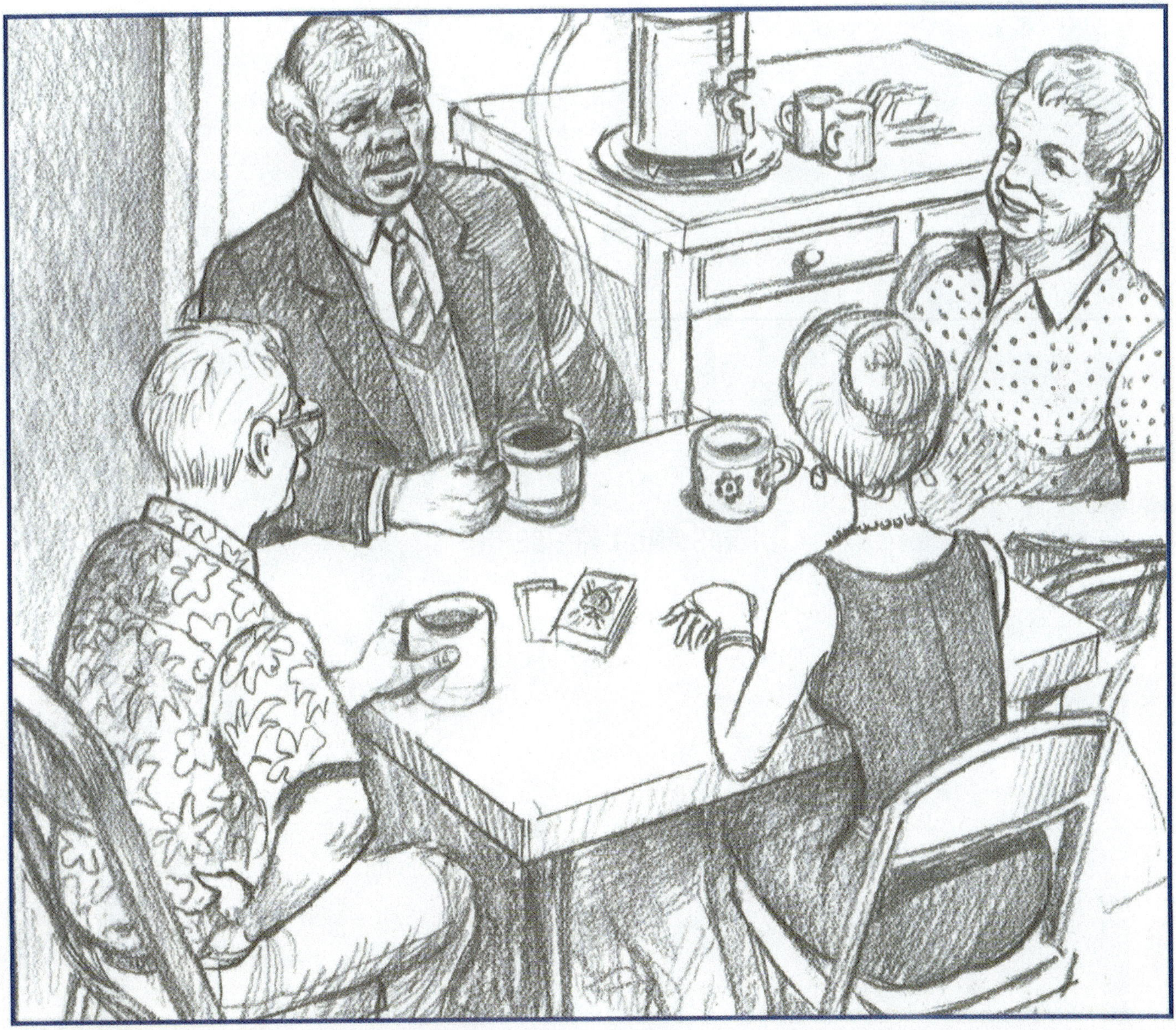

Vocabulary, Idioms, and Expressions

Practice pronouncing the following list of words and expressions. Then, take notes while your teacher gives the definitions.

Vocabulary

community center
bridge (game)
products
retire to survive
to lose or gain weight
defensively
heart attack
therapist
workaholic
to be productive
RV (recreational vehicle)
to mope
workout
aerobics
value
fragile
adorable

Idioms and Expressions

nothing better to do
That's the point!
just about to disappear
You're telling me!
one bit
Wake up!
to slow down
That's a joke!
big bucks
settle down
depend on
should know by now
to bounce back
You're only as young as you feel.
What's keeping (someone) so long?

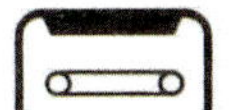

Dialogue

Prelistening

Discuss the following questions.

1. At what age do people in your country usually retire? What do people do after they retire?
2. How hard do people in your country work? How about in the U.S.? Give examples.
3. How are the elderly treated in your country? How about in the U.S.? Give examples.
4. Are people in your country usually dependent on family members? Are they generally independent? How about in the U.S.? Give examples.
5. How are pets treated in your country? How about in the U.S.? Give examples.
6. How conscious about their appearance and their health are people in your country? How about in the U.S.? Give examples.
7. Are people in your country very direct when they speak to others? How about in the U.S.? Give examples.

Dialogue

Listen to the following dialogue with your books closed. Take notes as you listen, so you can ask your teacher any questions you may have.

CAST OF CHARACTERS

MARY	**ROBIN**	**MICHAEL**
AL	**CAMERON**	

(These four friends are at their weekly bridge club meeting in the neighborhood community center.)

Michael: How's work, Al?

Al: Pretty good. I just got back from Dallas, and the new hospital there is very interested in our products. It looks like we are going to make big bucks there.

Michael: All you ever think of is money, isn't it? Don't you have enough yet? I know you could retire if you wanted to.

Mary: That's the point. He doesn't want to. He likes to keep busy. Robin, are you still losing weight? You're just about to disappear.

Robin: I only have five more pounds to go. This diet program I'm on is incredible. You should try it, Mary.

Mary: I don't need to lose weight. Anyway, my doctor says that I shouldn't lose or gain too much weight, especially after my heart attack last year. He said it might cause too much stress on my heart.

Michael: How have you been feeling, Mary?

Mary: Good. I don't know why everyone seems to think I'm so fragile. I'm just fine.

Michael: Oh, I almost forgot to tell you all. Trudy finally got pregnant!

Robin: You and that dog. I think you treat her better than you treat your own kids.

Michael: That's because Trudy respects and loves me more than my kids do.

Al: You're telling me. Do you know what Cameron said to me the other day? He told me that I needed a therapist. He doesn't respect me one bit for being so successful at what I do. He doesn't even appreciate that I started out with nothing, and that all my hard work was what made it possible for him to have things I didn't have. Now, he thinks I'm a workaholic.

Michael: Wake up, Al. You are a workaholic. You're going to kill yourself if you don't slow down. You're not a young man anymore, you know.

Al: You're only as young as you feel. I simply like to be productive. Unlike you, who has nothing better to do than to travel around in your RV with Trudy.

Mary: Come on, you guys. Settle down. Robin, did I tell you that my daughter, Jenny, wants me to come live with her? She is getting worried that I might die soon.

Robin: Ha! That's a joke! She should know by now that you will never depend on another person. I can't believe how well you have bounced back since Fred's death.

Mary: I'm not going to mope forever.

Robin: You are so strong, Mary. You have survived so much. I really admire you.

Mary: Thanks, Robin. It's getting late. Let's go play cards, people.

(Several weeks later, at another bridge club meeting)

Mary: Did you just get back from aerobics, Robin?

Robin: Yeah, I had a great workout.

Mary: How often are you exercising these days?

Robin: Five days a week. And I feel so good. I have so much energy that I didn't used to have. And even more importantly, I'm now a size six.

Michael: Hey, girls. Have you been waiting long?

Mary: No, just about 10 minutes.

Michael: Well, I'm now the proud grandpa of seven beautiful puppies. They're so adorable. And Trudy is doing so well, too.

Robin: You're kidding! Congratulations.

Michael: I know you both are going to want one. Why don't you come over this afternoon and see them. I wonder what's keeping Al so long. He's never late.

Mary: Let me give him a call, because I'm taking my grandkids to the park this afternoon, and I don't want to be late.

(On the phone)

Cameron: Hello.

Mary: Hi. Is Al there?

Cameron: No. Who's calling?

Mary: This is Mary, one of his bridge partners.

Cameron: Oh, hi Mary. This is Cameron. My father had a heart attack this morning. He's at State Memorial Hospital right now. He's okay, but the doctor has told him he'll have to quit his job.

Comprehension

Answer the following questions without looking back at the dialogue. If necessary, listen to the dialogue again.

1. What does Al do?
2. Why doesn't Al want to retire?
3. Does Mary think that Robin needs to keep losing weight?
4. What "things" do you think Al's son had that Al didn't have?
5. How do Michael and Al's values differ?
6. What do Michael and Al's children have in common?
7. What do you think Mary values the most in her life? Give examples.
8. What do you think Robin values the most in her life? Give examples.
9. What do you think caused Al's heart attack?

Language Focus

Read and Study

Many speakers have problems with pronouncing **[r]** and **[l]**.

To pronounce **[r]**, raise your tongue and curl the sides. The tip of your tongue should be close to the gum ridge. The sides of your tongue should press against the sides of your teeth. Round your lips and make the **[r]** sound for the words below.

respect	aerobics	admire
Robin	stress	forever
pretty	therapist	products
grandkids	worried	bridge

In order to pronounce **[l]**, the tip of your tongue should touch the upper gum ridge behind the upper front teeth. The sides of your tongue should be touching your lower back teeth. Your lips are relaxed, not rounded. Make the **[l]** sound for the following words.

long	workaholic	Dallas
late	hello	unlike
let	especially	believe
lose	tell	memorial

Language Focus Activity

One student reads sentence a or b. Another student circles the sentence he or she heard.

1. **a.** My father works for a **tile** company.

   b. My father works for a **tire** company.

2. **a.** Did you hear about the **crime** in the mountains?

   b. Did you hear about the **climb** in the mountains?

3. **a.** He's **playing** near the **rake**.

   b. He's **praying** near the **lake**.

4. **a.** That green **grass** is beautiful.

   b. That green **glass** is beautiful.

5. **a.** Do you know how to **lead**?

   b. Do you know how to **read**?

Vocabulary Activities

Vocabulary Activity 1 MATCHING

Put the letter of the correct word or words next to the appropriate statements.

1. __f__ to feel sorry for yourself		a. one bit
2. ____ to stop working and enjoy life		b. products
3. ____ easily hurt or broken		c. big bucks
4. ____ a person who counsels people		d. bounce back
5. ____ exercise		e. to be productive
6. ____ I agree with you.		f. to mope
7. ____ very cute		g. You're telling me!
8. ____ to recover or get well		h. value
9. ____ at all		i. fragile
10. ____ calm down		j. settle down
11. ____ items purchased		k. workout
12. ____ something important to a person		l. community center
13. ____ a place where people can do things together		m. retire
14. ____ to use time doing something useful		n. therapist
15. ____ a lot of money		o. adorable

Vocabulary Activity 2 VOCABULARY STORIES

In groups, write short stories. Use the following groups of words.

Group 1	Group 2	Group 3
bridge	heart attack	to work out
community center	therapist	aerobics
retire	workaholic	value
RV	slow down	to lose/gain weight
big bucks	to bounce back	one bit

Example: I have been a workaholic all my life. So, after I retired, I wanted to slow down and enjoy life more. I decided to buy an RV, and I wanted the best RV on the market. I didn't feel guilty one bit for spending big bucks on the best RV.

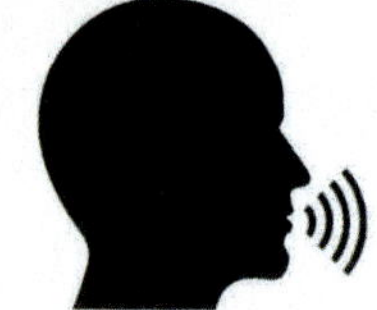

Speaking Activities

Speaking Activity 1 VALUES DISCUSSION

Below are some things in life that Americans value. Discuss why you think they are important to Americans. Give examples. Also, discuss any values you feel are different in your country.

Values:	Examples:
Individualism/ Independence	*leaving home at an early age (e.g. 18), couples having separate bank accounts, etc.*
Equality	
Time	
Change	
Wealth	
Youth	
Pets	
Work	
Honesty/Directness	

What other things do you think Americans value? How about in your culture?

Speaking Activity 2 SHORT TAKES

Read the dialogues below and decide which value from Speaking Activity 1 is being discussed. Then, finish the dialogue with a partner. Do you think these are typical American conversations?

1. A: What do you do in your free time?

   B: Usually, I cook for my family or clean up around the house.

   A: Do you ever just sit and watch TV or read a book?

   B: If I watch TV, I usually fold clothes or do work at the same time.

   A: ______________________________

   B: ______________________________

Value being discussed: ______________________________

2. A: I can't believe you don't pay for your girlfriend when you go out on a date.

   B: She works, so she pays for herself.

   A: I guess that makes sense.

   B: She likes to pay for herself.

   A: ______________________________

   B: ______________________________

Value being discussed: ______________________________

3. A: Where does Buck usually sleep?

   B: In my bed with me.

   A: He's just like your kid.

   B: I know.

   A: ______________________________

   B: ______________________________

Value being discussed: ______________________________

4. A: Could you please type these letters for me this afternoon?

   B: I have too much to do already. Is tomorrow soon enough?

   A: No, I need them today.

   B: Well, maybe someone else can help you.

   A: ______________________________

   B: ______________________________

Value being discussed: ______________________________

5. A: Have you used the new face cream I bought?

   B: Yeah, look how smooth my skin is now.

   A: I know. It's a miracle cream.

   B: ____

Value being discussed: ____

Speaking Activity 3 WORLD RELIGIONS

Together with your classmates, fill out the graph below with different religions from around the world. Then, write the values, beliefs, and practices of those religions. Unless you have a class with students from many different religions, you might have to do a little research for this activity, and perhaps some interviewing.

Religions:	Values, Beliefs, and Practices

Speaking Activity 4 SUPERSTITIONS GAME

The following game can be played individually or in teams. The game is timed. To start the game, each player or team will need a marker placed on the "Home" square. For each turn, move only one space along the lines in any direction. If you choose to move to the "Home" square, you lose that turn. For each circle, say as many superstitions as you know about for that topic. Example: Numbers — Number 13 is bad luck. For each superstition you come up with, you get one point. You can't repeat superstitions that another team or player has already named. The player or team who finishes with the most superstitions wins the game.
What superstitions do you know about?

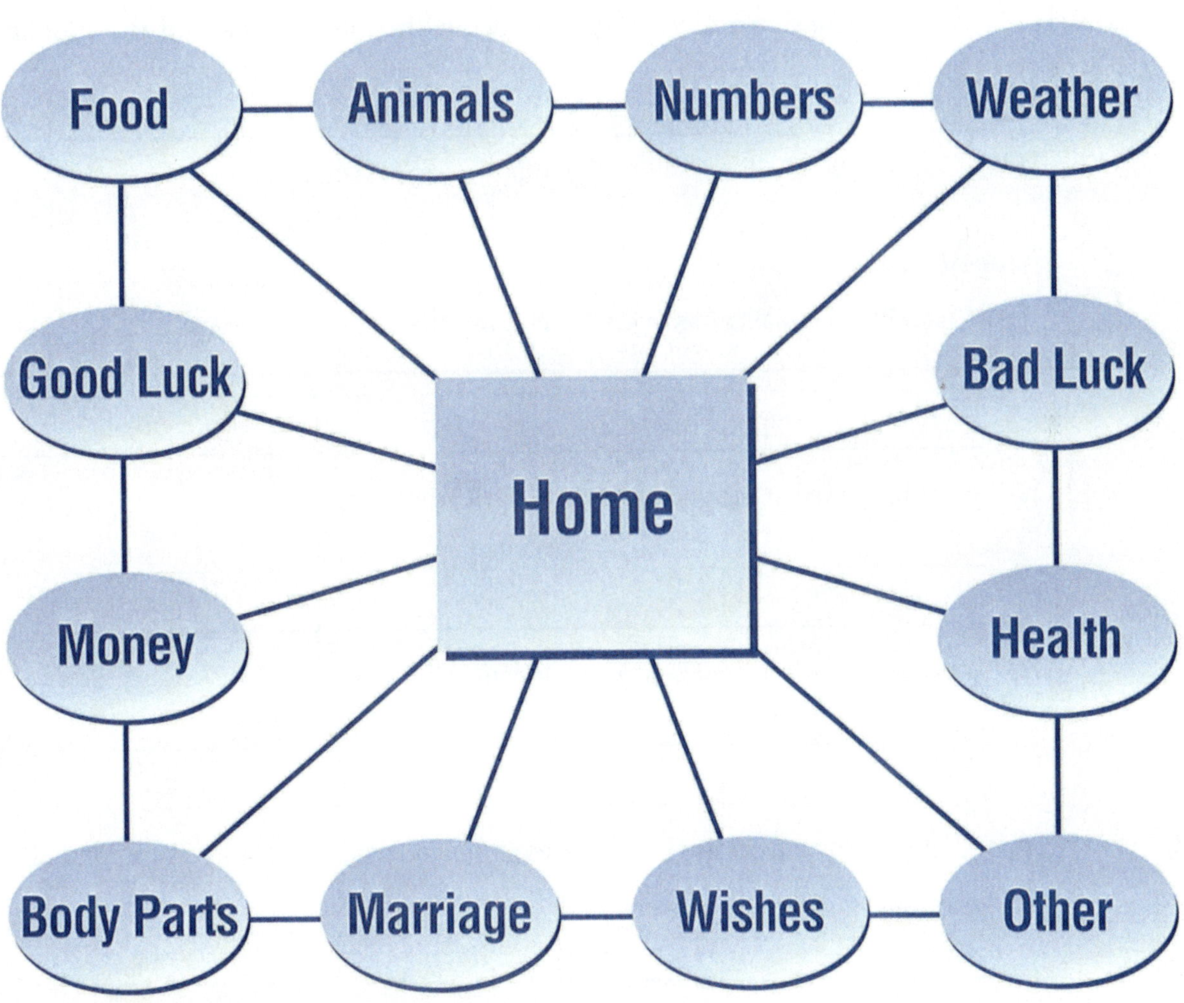

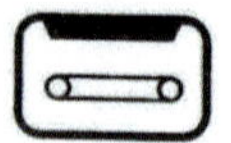

Listening Activity

LECTURE AND TIMELINE

Discuss the vocabulary below, then listen to the lecture. As you listen, fill out the timeline below, then answer the questions.

What do the following words mean?

discrimination	segregation	ancestral
prejudice	civil war	legal affairs
race/racial issues	slavery	

Timeline: Write down the events that occur during the years on the timeline below.

______|__________|__________|__________|__________|__________|__________

1863 1880-1890 1939-1945 1956 1968

Questions

1. What kind of equality has been difficult to achieve over the years?

   ____

   ____

2. What happened at the end of the U.S. Civil War?

   ____

   ____

3. What form of discrimination continued after the U.S. Civil War?

   ____

   ____

4. What other groups in the U.S. have experienced discrimination? What kind of discrimination did they experience?

   ____

   ____

5. What questions were asked at the end of the lecture? How would you answer them?

   ____

   ____

Outdoor Activities

Brainstorming

Look at the pictures below. Read and answer these questions:

Where are these people? What are they doing?

What is their relationship to each other? What are they talking about?

Vocabulary, Idioms, and Expressions

Practice pronouncing the following list of words and expressions. Then, take notes while your teacher gives the definitions.

VOCABULARY

fishing rod
bait
sunscreen
cooler
waves
sea gulls
bikini
sunburn
borrow
life jacket
to anchor
to cast out
hook
fishing line
to reel it in
net
mosquito bites
itch
scratch
insect repellent
to bark
to knock
hard of hearing
spoiled

IDIOMS AND EXPRESSIONS

Tell me about it!
to lie out in the sun
on sale
put on
to bet
dig in like crazy
to kill me
to take a look
to pass

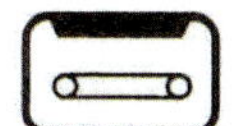

Dialogue

Prelistening

Discuss the following questions.

1. Did you ever go to the beach or a lake for a vacation?
2. Has your vacation ever been spoiled by sunburn or insect bites?
3. Do you like to lie out in the sun? Why or why not?
4. Have you ever been on a boat? What did you do on the boat? Did you enjoy it?
5. As a child, were you ever scared because your parents left you home alone?

Dialogue

Listen to the following dialogue with your books closed. Take notes as you listen, so you can ask your teacher any questions you may have.

CAST OF CHARACTERS

BALA HARI, PARVIN HARI, AND THEIR KIDS, RAM AND AMI

LANCE SMITH, ANDREA SMITH, AND THEIR KIDS, CATE AND ANDREW

(Two families from the same neighborhood are spending a three-day weekend at their vacation beach houses, which are next door to each other.)

Bala: Lance, what do you think about taking the kids out on the boat today?

Lance: Sounds great. I've got fishing rods for everybody.

Bala: Good. We'll just stop on the way to pick up some bait.

Lance: I'll go get the kids. I think they're all down on the beach.

(15 minutes later)

Andrea: Andrew, make sure you and Cate put on some sunscreen before you get on the boat.

Andrew: Okay. Mom, come here for a minute. I've got mosquito bites everywhere, and they itch like crazy.

Andrea: Well, don't scratch them. It will only make it worse.

Cate: Mom, do we have any insect repellent?

Andrea: I think so. Ask your Dad. Do you have mosquito bites, too?

Cate: Yes, and they're killing me.

Andrea: Hi Parvin. I'm coming down to the beach in just a minute.

Parvin: Great. Do you have any medicine for mosquito bites? Ram and Ami are covered with bites.

Andrea: So are my kids!

(The Dads and kids have left for their fishing trip. Parvin and Andrea are lying on the beach.)

Parvin: Now, this is a real vacation — no kids and no husbands. Just the sound of the waves and sea gulls flying above us.

Andrea: Tell me about it. It feels so good just to lie out in the sun.

Parvin: Hey, is that a new bikini?

Andrea: Yeah. I got it on sale at the new store near our house.

Parvin: It looks great on you. Could you pass me a soda out of the cooler?

Andrea: Sure. Here you go. Will you look at my back? Is it getting red?

Parvin: A little. Use my sunscreen. You don't want to get a sunburn.

(On the boat)

Bala: Everybody has to wear a life jacket. Ami, where is your life jacket?

Ami: I'm going to put it on. Just wait a minute. I have to scratch first.

Lance: All four of you have little red dots all over. The mosquitoes must think you're sweet.

Andrew: Very funny, Dad. Can I drive the boat, Mr. Hari?

Bala: Sure, come over here. I'll show you how to do it.

(Half an hour later)

Lance: This looks like a good spot. I bet there are a lot of fish here.

Ami: Let's anchor here, Dad.

Ram: I don't want to bait my hook. Will you do it for me, Dad?

Bala: No, to be a real fisherman, you have to bait your own hook.

Cate: I'll do it for you, Ram, if you will scratch my back. I can't reach the middle of my back.

Andrew: I'm casting my line out.

(A few minutes later)

Ram: I got one! Oh, my gosh. It's huge.

Bala: Reel it in. Good job. I can see it now. It's big.

Ram: Get the net.

Lance: I got it.

(Later that night)

Parvin: This fish looks delicious.

Ami: That's the one I caught. It's the biggest one.

Ram: It is not.

Andrea: It's ready now. Come to the table and dig in.

Andrew: I don't think the repellent is working. I have about 50 million more bites than I did this morning.

Lance: Come over here and let me take a look at them.

(The next evening, the adults go out for dinner, leaving the kids at home alone.)

Cate: It's so windy and dark outside. Do you know what time Mom and Dad are coming home, Andrew?

Andrew: They'll be home after you go to sleep. Why, are you scared?

Cate: No, but why do you think the dog is barking?

Andrew: He's probably just playing with the Hari's dog, or with Ami and Ram next door. Don't worry.

Cate: Listen, someone is coming up the stairs outside.

Andrew: Who is it?

Andrew: Who is it?

Cate: Why don't they answer?

Andrew: I don't know. I think we should go out the back and run over to Ram and Ami's.

(They run next door and tell Ram and Ami what has happened.)

Ram: Hey, listen. There's somebody at our door now.

Ami: Don't open the door!

Cate: I'm hiding under the bed.

Andrew: Do you have a baseball bat?

Ram: Yeah, it's in my room. Let's turn off all the lights.

(A couple hours later)

Lance: Cate and Andrew, what are you doing at the Hari's house? Shouldn't you be in bed?

(They tell their parents what happened.)

Lance: Oh, I forgot to tell you. My friend, Dr. Madden, who is hard of hearing, was bringing over some medicine for your mosquito bites.

Comprehension

Answer the following questions without looking back at the dialogue. If necessary, listen to the dialogue again.

1. Who goes fishing?
2. What do the mothers do?
3. Why do you think Ram doesn't want to bait his hook?
4. Who catches the first fish?
5. Does Andrew get 50 million mosquito bites?
6. At first, what three things scare Cate?
7. Why do Cate and Andrew run over to the Hari's house?
8. Why do the kids turn off the lights?
9. Why didn't the man answer when Andrew asked, "Who is it?"

Language Focus

Read and Study

Two-word verbs are verbs combined with prepositions that have a particular meaning that is different from that of the verb by itself (**get on = to board or get on top of something**). There are two types of two-word verbs: separable and inseparable.

<u>**Separable two-word verbs**</u> can be separated by nouns or object pronouns. Look at these examples from the dialogue.

1. What do you think about **taking** the kids **out** on the boat today?
2. Make sure you and Cate **put** some sunscreen **on**.
3. We'll just stop on the way to **pick** some bait **up**.
   (Notice that separable two-word verbs don't have to be separated if a noun is the object.)
4. We'll just stop on the way to **pick up** some bait.
   (However, if the verb is separated by a pronoun, it must be separated.)
5. I'm going to **put** it **on**. (Not *I'm going to put on it.)

<u>**Inseparable two-word verbs**</u> cannot be separated by any words and must always be followed by an object. Look at these examples from the dialogue.

1. **Get on** the boat. (Not, *Get the boat on.)
2. It feels good to **lie out** in the sun. (Not, *It feels good to lie in the sun out.)
3. **Come over** here and let me **look at** them. (Not, *Come here over and let me look them at.)

Language Focus Activity

Complete the sentences below, using a two-word verb and an object pronoun.

them	**her**	**it**	**him**	**pick out**	**look up**
write down	**throw away**	**look after**	**run into**	**go over**	

1. I don't know this word, so I have to ____________________ in the dictionary.
2. I have a younger sister. I usually ______________________________.
3. I can't believe I saw my old friend at the store.
   It was so nice to ____________________.
4. I don't need these papers. Would you ____________________ for me.
5. I need to study the vocabulary words one more time. I'll ____________________
   ____________________ before I go to bed tonight.
6. I can't remember the directions to your house. Would you give them to me one more time, so I can ______________________________.
7. We need vegetables for the salad. Please go to the store and ____________________
   ____________________ for the salad.

Vocabulary Activities

Vocabulary Activity 1 ODD ONE OUT

Draw a line through the word that has a different meaning.

1. **borrow**	to use temporarily	to check out	~~lend~~
2. **to anchor**	to leave	to stay	to tie up
3. **bikini**	underwear	swimming trunks	two-piece bathing suit
4. **spoiled**	ruined	rotten	fresh
5. **to bet**	to have a feeling	to say	to guess
6. **to dig in**	to eat	to put	to help yourself
7. **to pass**	to faint	to throw	to give
8. **net**	string knotted together	the divider in the middle of a tennis court	paper
9. **hook**	to lose	to catch	a tool with a curved end
10. **sunburn**	red skin	blisters	sunbathe

Vocabulary Activity 2 VOCABULARY BASEBALL

Divide the class into two teams. One team goes "up to bat" while the other team "pitches." The members of the pitching team take turns pitching words or expressions to members of the batting team. The batter chooses one of the four activities listed below after hearing the word. If the batter answers incorrectly, he or she gets a strike. After three strikes, the batter is out. After three outs, the other team comes to bat.

1. Spell the word or expression correctly and go to first base.
2. Give a definition of the word and go to second base.
3. Use the word correctly in a sentence and go to third base.
4. Do all of the three activities above and score a home run for your team.

Speaking Activities

Speaking Activity 1a AN OUTING WITH YOUR CLASSMATES

In groups of three or four, tell about the following outdoor activities that you can do where you live. After you tell about an activity, place a check mark √ next to it. Then find out the names of the places where you can do them.

Camping _____	Place ______________________________
Hiking _____	Place ______________________________
Beach _____	Place ______________________________
Fishing _____	Place ______________________________
Park or Zoo _____	Place ______________________________
City tour _____	Place ______________________________
Adventurous activities _____	Place ______________________________
Horseback riding _____	Place ______________________________
Other activities _____	Place ______________________________

Speaking Activity 1b AN OUTING WITH YOUR CLASSMATES

Work as a group to decide on one outdoor activity that you like and plan a trip. Present the trip idea to your class. After all the groups have presented their ideas, the whole class votes on the outing that sounds like the most fun. Follow the guidelines provided below in presenting your idea.

1. Describe the place you are planning to visit.
2. How will you get to this place?
3. What do you need to take with you?
4. What fun activities are you planning to do? Explain the activities.
5. When will you return?

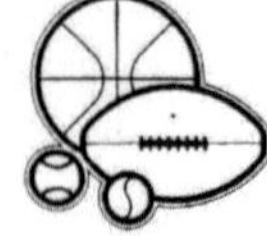

Speaking Activity 2 SPORTS

In teams, list all the vocabulary words associated with the sports listed below. Then, whichever team has the most vocabulary words for one particular sport explains the sport and shows how to play it, using all the words they listed. The team writes the words on the blackboard so that the class can check to see if the team is using all the words.

Swimming	Baseball	Football	Soccer
swimsuit *goggles* *bathing cap* *towel* *lap* *stroke* *dive*			

Skiing	Tennis	Golf	Basketball

Other	Hockey	Cycling	Other

Speaking Activity 3 FINDING DIFFERENCES

Work in pairs to find the differences in the following illustrations.

Partner A looks at this page while partner B looks at the next page. Partner A describes one thing about the picture. Partner B sees if that description matches his or her picture. If it does not match, then Partner B explains what it is that is different. Keep going until you have found all the differences.

Partner A

Speaking Activity 3 FINDING DIFFERENCES

Partner B

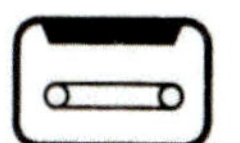

Listening Activity

Listening Activity 1a DRAW WHAT YOU HEAR

Listen to the description of an outdoor scene on tape. Draw what you hear in the box below. Then, compare your drawings with your classmates' drawings. You don't have to be an artist. Simple drawings are fine.

Listening Activity 1b DRAW WHAT YOU HEAR

Draw any outdoor scene in one of the boxes below. Describe your scene to your partner. Then, listen to your partner's description and draw what you hear. Compare the two drawings and tell how they are different.

Your Drawing	Your Partner's Description

Jobs and Business

Brainstorming

Look at the pictures below. Read and answer these questions: What are the people in the pictures doing? What are they talking about? What are their jobs?

Vocabulary, Idioms, and Expressions

Practice pronouncing the following list of words and expressions. Then, take notes while your teacher gives the definitions.

Vocabulary

field
current
to label
listing
position
specific
job opening
stockbroker
barely
potential
clientele/client
transcript
Wall Street
share
competitive
portfolio
resume
to handle
profit
loss
impressive
account executive

Idioms and Expressions

to build up
to make ends meet
to manage
for that matter
get a life
to work like a dog

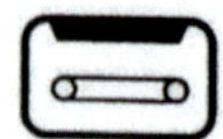

Dialogue

Prelistening

Discuss the following questions.

1. Do you have career centers in colleges and universities in your country? If so, tell about the services they provide for students. If not, ask other students about career centers in their countries, or in U.S. institutions.
2. What kinds of jobs are you interested in? Explain why?
3. What are some common questions asked in job interviews?
4. What are the advantages and disadvantages of working in business or finance?
5. Is it common for people to change careers in your country? Why do some people change careers?

Dialogue

Listen to the following dialogue with your books closed. Take notes as you listen, so you can ask your teacher any questions you may have.

CAST OF CHARACTERS

VAL	**KATIE**
COLE	**SHAAFI**

(In the career center of a college campus)

Katie: Can I help you with anything?

Val: Yes, I would like to look at some job listings.

Katie: In what field?

Val: Finance or business.

Katie: All right. All the current job listings are located on the bottom shelf over in the corner. Just look in the binder labeled "B" for business or "F" for finance. Let me know if I can help you with anything after you have looked at the listings.

Val: Can I ask a question?

Katie: Sure.

Val: Do the listings normally have the starting salaries on them?

Katie: Some of them do. Sometimes you actually have to call to find out the details of the position.

Val: I see. Thank you.

(Several minutes later)

Val: Excuse me. Could I ask you a few questions about these specific jobs?

Katie: Yes. I'll be with you in just a moment.

Katie: Okay. How can I help you?

Val: Well, I've found a couple job openings that look interesting, but I'd like to have your professional opinion. Which position do you feel would be more profitable, a stockbroker's position, or an account executive for a good company?

Katie: Profitable? That depends. I know of some graduates who have made quite a bit as stockbrokers and others who just barely made ends meet.

Val: How about the account executive?

Katie: Well, beginning salaries aren't that high, but the potential is good.

Val: So, stockbrokers can make more money to begin with, right?

Katie: They can, but they usually have to work a lot of overtime in the beginning, until they have built up a good clientele.

Val: I think that's the job for me. What's a few hours of overtime?

(At the interview)

Cole: So, you are graduating when?

Val: In June.

Cole: Well, your transcript looks good. Tell me about why you want to be a stockbroker.

Val: I feel it would be a very exciting career. I love to watch the brokers on Wall Street buying and selling shares.

Cole: It is exciting. Do you think you're competitive enough for the job?

Val: Oh, yes. I've always been a competitive person. Did you see there that I placed in the top 10 in the New York City Marathon last year?

Cole: Yes, that's very impressive. I also see here on your resume that you worked part-time for the accounting department at an insurance agency. What were your responsibilities there?

Val: I handled all client payments. I really learned about accounting.

Cole: Good. I think you'd do a fine job here. I'd like to offer you the job on a temporary basis, and then after 90 days we will check your portfolio to see how many clients you have been able to get. If you meet our requirements within 90 days, we'll give you a permanent position.

(After a month on the job, Val is talking to his friend and coworker.)

Val: Morning, Shaafi.

Shaafi: Hey, Val. I guess you're feeling good after yesterday. How do you manage to pick all the best stocks?

Val: I guess I'm just lucky, except for in love. I don't have any time to date or do anything else for that matter.

Shaafi: Yeah, but I saw your new car. I guess you won't have any problems finding dates from now on.

Val: Shaafi, get a life. Seriously, Shaafi, I've been thinking. Even the brokers who have been here awhile are working like dogs. I don't think this is worth all the money.

Shaafi: I can't believe what I'm hearing. YOU don't think it's worth the money.

Val: Yeah, money is not everything. I made a decision last night.

Shaafi: What?

Val: I'm giving my notice today. I'm going to look for an easier job, like the track coach at the high school.

Shaafi: You've got to be kidding.

Comprehension

Answer the following questions without looking back at the dialogue. If necessary, listen to the dialogue again.

1. What seems most important to Val in his job search?
2. What information does Katie give Val that helps him make his decision?
3. Was Val a good student? Explain.
4. Why do you think Cole hired Val for the job?
5. How does Val do in his first month working as a stockbroker?
6. Do you think Shaafi does as well as Val as a stockbroker? Explain.
7. How does Val's point of view change after a month on the job?
8. Give two reasons why Val probably wants to be a track coach.

Language Focus

Read and Study

Many speakers have problems with pronouncing **[p]** and **[f]**.

To pronounce **[p]**, press your lips together, and then release them with a strong puff of air.

To pronounce **[f]**, put your upper front teeth gently on your lower lip. Without moving your teeth, let out a stream of air. Practice saying the words below with your teacher.

pace	face	pour	four	step	Steph
peel	feel	leapt	left	leap	leaf
pile	file	copy	coffee	beep	beef
pool	fool	open	often	lap	laugh
pine	fine	cheap	chief		

Language Focus Activity

Read the passage below into a tape. Exchange your tape with a classmate, and listen to his or her tape. Circle the **[f]** or **[p]** sounds that your classmate has trouble with. Then, return the tape. Practice as many times as necessary.

Note: You can focus on other sounds that give you trouble in the passage, too.

Steph, look at what the gardener did. He left a pile of leaves right in front of my car. I often tell him to put the leaves on the side of the house, but he just laughs. Now, I have to beep my horn to get his attention. What's he doing now? That fool is cleaning the pool. He can't hear me because he's wearing headphones. I feel so frustrated. I guess it's not his fault. I'll just open my trunk and put the leaves in and take them to the dump. Maybe this is why this gardener is so cheap. I have to pay more for full-service gardening.

Vocabulary Activities

Vocabulary Activity 1 SHOW ME THE MONEY!

Play the following game in small groups, or teams. Two teams or two players compete. One person is the game host. Decide which person or team will go first. Choose a category and a dollar amount. The host reads a sentence, and the other player has 30 seconds to give the appropriate response. If your response is correct, you get the money for that square. If your response is wrong, you owe that amount. The player or team with the most money at the end of the game is the winner.

Miscellaneous	Business	Idioms	The Job Search
$100	$100	$100	$100
$200	$200	$200	$200
$300	$300	$300	$300
$400	$400	$400	$400
$500	$500	$500	$500

Vocabulary Activity 2 VOCABULARY PYRAMIDS

Write words that are related to the words in each pyramid. In a complete sentence, tell how each word relates to the word in the pyramid.

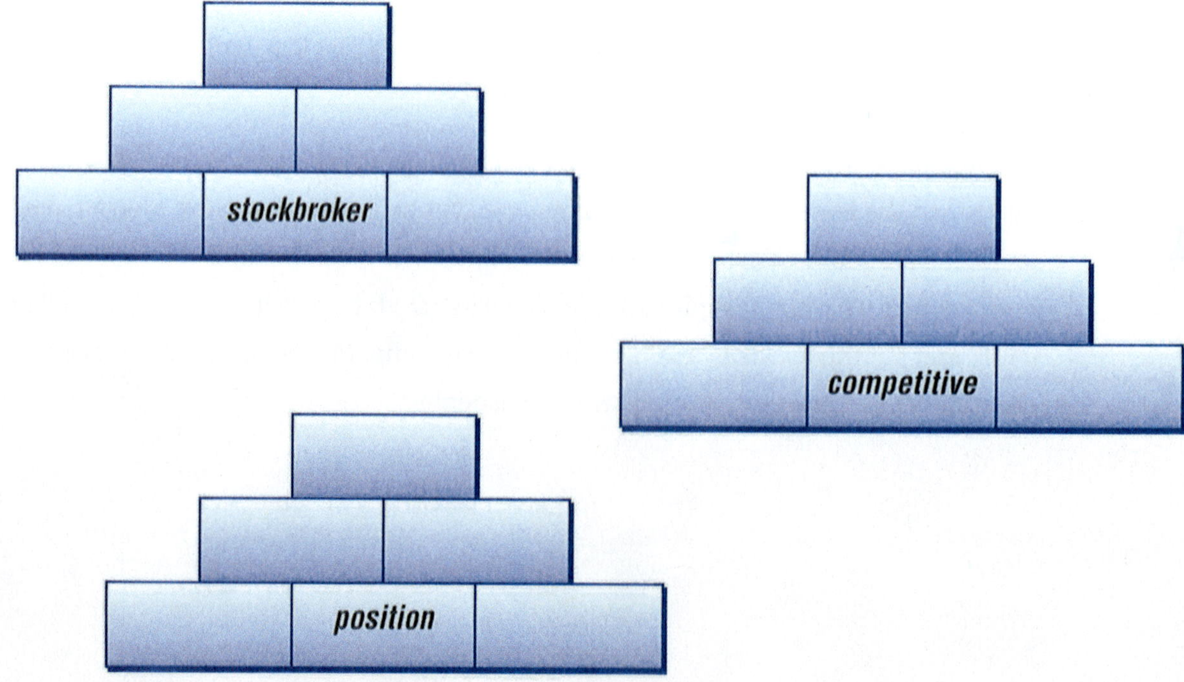

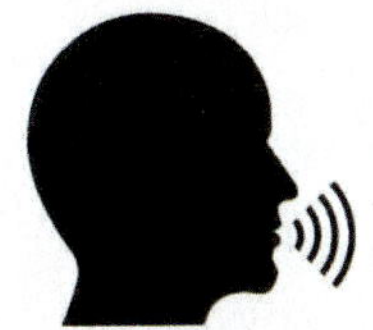

Speaking Activities

Speaking Activity 1 WORK EXPERIENCE

Discuss the following topics.

1. What part-time or full-time jobs have you had? Were you paid by the hour?
2. Is it common for students to work in your country?
3. What was the worst job you have ever had? Explain.
4. What was the best job you have ever had? Explain.
5. What are some jobs you think you would enjoy? Explain.
6. What are some jobs you think you wouldn't enjoy? Explain.
7. What experience, education, or training will you need before you find your ideal job?
8. In the U.S., it is illegal to discriminate on the basis of race, religion, age, or sex when hiring a person for a job. So certain questions cannot be asked during an interview. What do you think those questions might be?

Speaking Activity 2 ASPECTS OF A JOB

Look at the list below. What things are important to you in choosing a job? Circle the five most important things and cross out the five least important things. Compare your choices with the choices of other students. Explain your choices.

salary
health benefits
retirement and investment benefits
vacation
job security
advancement opportunities
distance from home (commute)
stress level
number of work hours
challenging work
a nice office
day-care service
fitness program provided by employer
independence on the job
free parking
friendly coworkers
a fair supervisor
high status
professional development
recognition, awards, and raises
travel opportunities
varied responsibilities
casual work place
working outside
physical work
bonuses

Speaking Activity 3 JOB LISTINGS

Based on your answers in Activity 1, choose a job from the listings below, or from the newspaper. Explain why you have chosen this job. Also, discuss what the following may mean: F/T, P/T, K, incl., xlnt, pref, nec., exp., EOE, AA, reqd., @, and min.

Accountant
For a publishing company. F/T, assisting with various accounting projects. Must know computers. 27-31K, benefits incl.
Fax resume to (876) 435-9869.

Veterinary Technician
Friendly person needed for a busy 5 doctor practice. Exp. pref.
Must apply in person.
Call (238) 987-2343 for details.

High School English Teacher
Teaching credential reqd.
Send resume to: Sierra Grande Unified School District,
PO Box 675,
Sierra Grande, CA 98789.

Hair stylist
Full-service family salon.
No previous clientele nec.
P/T or F/T.
Call (765) 876-8983.

Construction Foreman
Seeking person with good management skills. Must have min. 5 yrs. exp.
Call (765) 543-0987.

Chef
Min. 2 yrs. exp., to cook and prepare Italian specialty foods for independently operated, fine waterfront restaurant.
Call for more info. (454) 124-0987.

Computer Programmer
Two programmers wanted to develop software for banking systems.
Investment opportunities available.
Fax resume to (878) 762-4367.

Bartender
Wanted, F/T bartender for busy night shift. Apply in person.
@ 849 Oceanfront Ave.,
Victoria, MA 76488.

Mechanical Engineer
Mechanical engineers needed to design new equipment. Send resume to human resources @ PO Box 675, Boatsville, OH 87654. EOE AA employer.

Writer
For daily community newspaper. Interview, research, and write about events in the community. Future editing position available. 40K. Call (890) 767-2232.

Outside Sales
Achieve the financial success you've always wanted selling medical supplies. Some traveling nec. Hours flexible. Must be independent.
Call (901) 230-9065.

Executive Secretary
To the president of security system manufacturing company. Must have computer knowledge. xlnt $ + bonuses.
Call (909) 675-8873.

Speaking Activity 4 JOB INTERVIEWS

With a partner, talk about some questions you might be asked on an interview for the jobs you chose in Activity 3. Write the questions below. With your partner, role-play an interview.

1. ______________________________
2. ______________________________
3. ______________________________
4. ______________________________
5. ______________________________

Speaking Activity 5 DIPLOMACY AT WORK

Diplomacy means dealing with people with tact and calm. It means being polite. When speaking with coworkers or bosses, it's important to say things diplomatically.

Look at the following statements. They are not very diplomatic. How do you think the other person might respond? How can you change the statements so that they are diplomatic?

1. **Bob:** These papers are very important. Don't lose them like you did last time.

   Frank: ______________________________

   Diplomatic alternative:

   Bob: ______________________________

   Frank: ______________________________

2. **Denise:** Your suggestion is not good. We tried it that way before. It doesn't work.

   Barbara: ______________________________

   Diplomatic alternative:

   Denise: ______________________________

   Barbara: ______________________________

3. **Bill:** I don't have time to help you with the computer again today. I think you need to take a computer class.

   Susan: ______________________________

   Diplomatic alternative:

   Bill: ______________________________

   Susan: ______________________________

4. **Linda:** The reason you don't succeed is that you take too many coffee breaks.

   Martha:____

   Diplomatic alternative:

   Linda:____

   Martha:____

Speaking Activity 6 WORKING WORLD

Interview a native English speaker who works, preferably in the field you would like to work in. Bring your answers to class for a discussion.

1. Job ____________________ Company name ____________________
2. Why did you choose this job?

   ____
3. How long have you been working for this company?

   ____
4. What are your job responsibilities?

   ____
5. How many hours a week do you work?

   ____
6. Do you have regular breaks? If yes, when do you have breaks?

   ____
7. What benefits are you given?

   ____
8. Have you had other jobs or careers? What were they?

   ____
9. What is the best aspect of your job?

   ____
10. What is the worst aspect of your job?

    ____
11. (Ask your own question.)

    ____

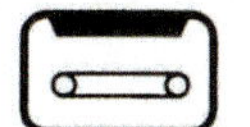

Listening Activity NOT A HAPPY CLIENT

Listen to the conversation that takes place between a loan agent and her supervisor. Then read the list below. Listen to the conversation again. Then listen to the questions about the conversation. Match the number of each question with one of the items listed below.

Jean is unhappy with her client.

Jean is unhappy with Shawn.

Jean's client

Jean's coworker

Jean's supervisor

Looking for a competitive loan. To work harder

Returning her client's calls.

Tell the client everything.

That it is Jean's fault.

That maybe Jean can focus on pleasing other clients.

That the client is hard to please.

The client is unhappy.

Upset and sorry to have lost the money.

CULTURAL NOTE: It's common in the United States to call bosses and supervisors by their first names. This is because Americans value equality, as discussed in Unit 9. In addition, Americans tend to be more informal than people in other cultures. Many workers in the U.S. call their bosses by their first names. They may dress casually on Fridays and treat clients and coworkers as friends rather than professional acquaintances. What is the work environment like in your country?

UNIT 12

Current Events

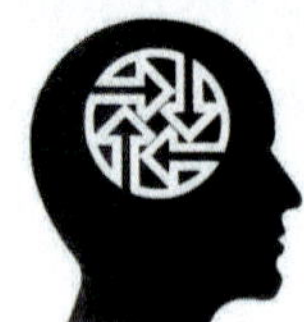

Brainstorming

Look at the picture below. Read and answer these questions:

What is the older man doing? Why? What do you think he just said?

What is the younger man doing? Why?

Vocabulary, Idioms, and Expressions

Practice pronouncing the following list of words and expressions. Then, take notes while your teacher gives the definitions.

Vocabulary

spare
change
to mug
desperate
to beg
rude
to doubt
alcoholic
to ruin
insensitive
stable
handicap
fortunate
city council
resident
vent
to provide
shelter
soup kitchen
to volunteer
to support
guy

Idioms and Expressions

to hang out / to hang around
to feel sorry for someone
a pretty cool person or thing
to swear (something)
the least (someone) can do

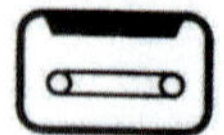

Dialogue

Prelistening

Discuss the following questions.

1. Are there many homeless people in your country or in your city?
2. How do you feel about homeless people? Explain.
3. Have you ever given money to a homeless person? Why or why not?
4. How does the government in your country help the homeless? How about in the U.S.?
5. What other types of programs have you heard of that support the homeless?
6. Have you ever seen homeless women or children?
7. How do you think people become homeless?

Dialogue

Listen to the following dialogue with your books closed. Take notes as you listen, so you can ask your teacher any questions you may have.

CAST OF CHARACTERS

SCOTT **KEITH**

(Scott and Keith are brothers who just recently moved from a small town in the U.S. to a big city.)

Keith: Hey, Scott, have you seen that homeless guy who hangs out in front of the supermarket?

Scott: Yeah.

Keith: Just the other day, he asked me for some spare change.

Scott: What did you do?

Keith: I was a little uncomfortable, so I just told him I didn't have any.

Scott: Why didn't you give him a quarter or something?

Keith: I don't know. I didn't really have time to think. I felt like if I had taken out my wallet, he would have mugged me or something.

Scott: Come on, Keith. He's not a criminal. He's just poor.

Keith: I know, but some of these guys are desperate. What do you do when they ask you for money?

Scott: I usually give them some.

Keith: That's the problem. I think these guys stay homeless because they can make money the easy way. They don't have to go out and get a job if people keep giving them change.

Scott: Oh, sure, Keith. The reason they beg is just because they're lazy.

Keith: Well...

Scott: Did you know that that homeless guy has a family?

Keith: How do you know that?

Scott: Because last weekend I saw him in front of the store with a woman and a baby.

Keith: I hate to be rude, but standing out there with them could just be a plan to make people feel sorry for them, you know?

Scott: I seriously doubt that, Keith.

Keith: I think a lot of homeless guys are alcoholics who have ruined their lives by drinking too much, and if you give them money, they will just go spend it on liquor.

Scott: Keith, you're so insensitive. How would you feel if you didn't have a job or a place to live?

Keith: I don't think I'd ever be in that situation. If I lost my job, I'd look until I found a new one. I know I would be able to find some work.

Scott: Well, not all people are as lucky as you. Some people don't have stable parents or a good education. They might even have mental problems or handicaps. They might need help from more fortunate people like you and me.

Keith: Whatever.

(Several days later: Scott and Keith have just come home from work.)

Scott: Hey. What's up?

Keith: Nothing. How was your day?

Scott: Not so good.

Keith: Why? What happened?

Scott: You know my boss, Dan?

Keith: Yeah, I met him at your company's party last year. He seemed like a pretty cool guy.

Scott: Well, he has a position on the city council. And I guess a lot of residents and business owners downtown are complaining about all the homeless. They hang out on the streets downtown because the warm air from the subways comes up through the vents. And they're trying to stay warm. Anyway, Dan and the other council members have decided to cover up the vents so they won't hang around there anymore.

Keith: Really!?

Scott: I'm really upset about this. I asked Dan if they also had plans to provide or build a shelter for them. And they don't.

Keith: Hmm.

(Several months later, in the middle of a cold winter.)

Scott: Well, I never see any homeless downtown anymore. I swear, I'm so mad at Dan.

Keith: What are you going to do?

Scott: I don't know, but I have to do something.

Keith: I know there's a soup kitchen on Main Street. Maybe that's where they've all gone.

Scott: You're probably right. I think I'll go down there right now and volunteer my time.

Keith: You know what? I'll go with you.

Scott: What! You!?

Keith: Yeah, I feel kind of bad that they all have to move after the council's decision. I know I don't support them on the streets. But helping to feed them is the least I can do. So, will you give me a ride downtown?

Scott: Of course. Come on. Let's go.

Comprehension

Answer the following questions without looking back at the dialogue. If necessary, listen to the dialogue again.

1. What does Keith do when the homeless guy asks him for money? Why?
2. How does Keith think people become homeless?
3. How does Scott think people become homeless?
4. Why is Scott so angry with his boss?
5. What do Keith and Scott decide to do at the end of the dialogue?
6. Why do you think Keith has changed his mind?

Language Focus

Read and Study

A noun clause often follows a complete sentence or a main clause. It serves as the object of the sentence. All noun clauses contain their own subject (S) and verb (V). Sometimes they begin with question words (*what, when, where, which, who, why, how*). Sometimes they begin with the word *if.* And sometimes they begin with an optional *that.* Look at the following examples from the dialogue.

	?-word S V
What do you do	when they ask you for money?
main clause	*noun clause/ object of sentence*

	that S V
I feel kind of bad	(that) they have to move.
main clause	*noun clause/ object of sentence*

	if S V
They don't have to go out and get a job	if people keep giving them change.
main clause	*noun clause/ object of sentence*

Language Focus Activity

Complete the following sentences using noun clauses.

1. Did you know (that) ______________________________?
2. I know where ______________________________.
3. I wonder if ______________________________.
4. I don't know what ______________________________.
5. I had a dream that ______________________________.
6. I want to know why ______________________________.
7. Ask our teacher if ______________________________.
8. Do you know who ______________________________?
9. She realizes (that) ______________________________.
10. Can you tell me how ______________________________?

Vocabulary Activity

CROSSWORD PUZZLE

Solve the crossword puzzle using the clues given below.

Across

5. impolite behavior or impolite words
7. a person who can't stop drinking because of alcoholism
8. to help
9. a person who lives in a certain area
11. a place where homeless people can sleep, eat, and feel safe
13. strong or dependable
16. not aware of other people's feelings
17. to destroy
18. to ask for food or money on the street
19. to attack someone with the intention of robbing him or her

Down

1. to be absolutely sure
2. lucky
3. to feel bad
4. coins
6. in great need
10. not sure
11. unused or extra
12. a person who agrees to do something without pay
14. a disability, either physical or emotional
15. an opening that is used to let hot air escape

Speaking Activities

Speaking Activity 1 PASS THE BUCK: CONTROVERSIAL ISSUES

Before starting this activity, make sure you understand all the vocabulary words and the issues below. Ask your teacher if you have any questions. Divide the class into small groups. Each group takes out a dollar bill or play money. One person takes the dollar bill and discusses the first issue. She or he can talk about problems, solutions, and/or opinions related to the issue. Others in the class can agree or disagree with the speaker. Then, the speaker passes the buck to the next person, who discusses the next issue.

1. Prostitution
2. Women in society
3. Sex, violence, and profanity on TV and in the movies
4. "Pulling the plug"/Euthanasia
5. Animal rights
   Animals in research
6. Drugs
   Should drugs be legal or illegal?
7. Alcoholism
8. Cigarette Smoking
9. Abortion
10. Life in Space
11. Terrorism/Bombings
12. Police brutality
13. Homeless
14. Other

Speaking Activity 2 DEBATE

Choose an issue from Speaking Activity 1 that your class thought was the most controversial. Divide the class into two groups. The groups have different opinions about the issue. Along with your group, list the arguments that support your opinion. Decide who will present each argument. Then, guess how the other group will try to counter your argument. Finally, think of a way to defend your argument against their counterargument. Now you are ready to debate.

Issue to be debated ______________________________

Opposing opinions about the issue:

a) ______________________________

b) ______________________________

Your group's point of view ______________________________

1. Who will present each argument	2. Arguments to support your point of view	3. How the other group will counter your argument	4. What you will say to their counterargument

Speaking Activity 3 WAYS TO SAVE THE ENVIRONMENT

In small groups, take turns rolling two dice. Look at the picture in the square that matches the number on the dice. Tell your group how you can use this object (or use it less) to help save the environment.

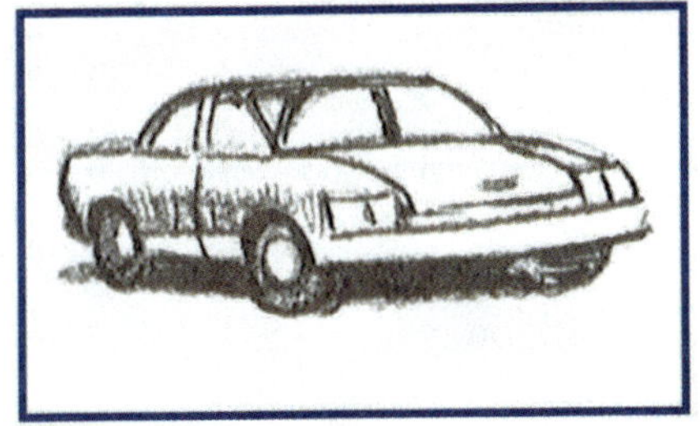

1

2

3

4

5

6

7

8

9

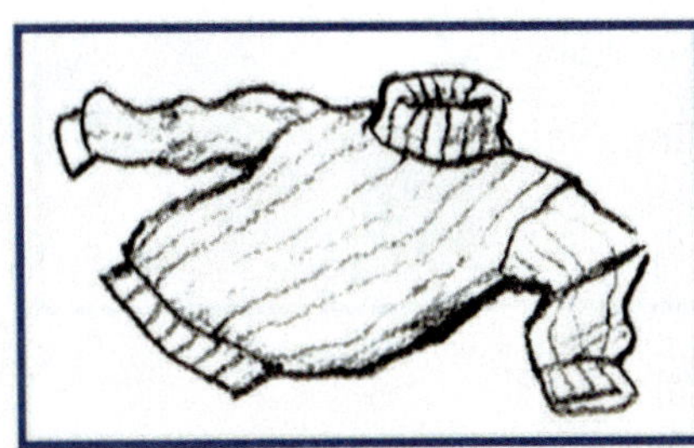

10

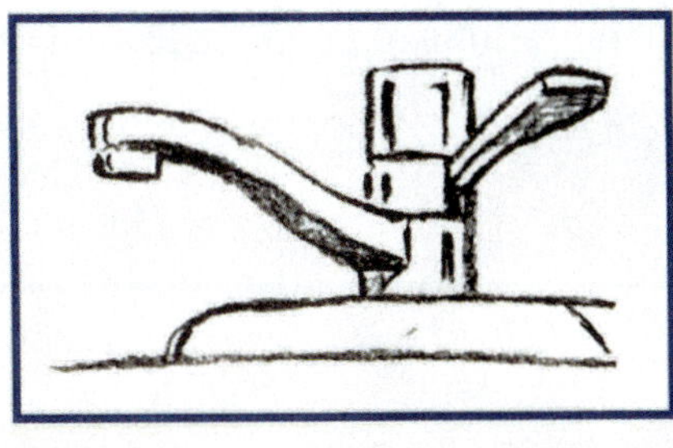

11

12

Speaking Activity 4 THE WAVE OF THE FUTURE

Discuss the following questions:

1. How is AIDS affecting our society today?
   Do you think there will be a cure for AIDS in the near future? Explain.
   If there is no cure, what do you think will happen?

2. What country has the most powerful nuclear weapons in the world today?
   If one of those weapons were used, what do you think would happen?
   Do you think that the world will ever be rid of nuclear weapons?

3. Are there any wars occurring in the world today? If so, where?
   What are the people involved fighting over?
   Do you think people will ever find a way to stop fighting? How?

4. In what areas of the world are people starving?
   Do you think we will ever find a way to wipe out hunger all over the world? How?

5. Do you think computers will cause a shortage of jobs for people in the future? How?
   Do you think computers and technology will cause any problems in the future? Explain.

6. Where are large migrations happening in the world today?
   Why are these people on the move?
   How do you think large migrations of people will affect the future?
   Are there any solutions to the problems these people are facing in their native countries?

Listening Activity

CLASS DISCUSSION

Listen to the discussion that takes place in a social science class. Answer the questions that follow the discussion.

1. What is the topic of this class discussion?

____

____

____

____

2. List the subtopics that the students bring up.

____

____

____

____

____

____

3. Why is the professor surprised when Leonid gives a good answer at the end of the discussion?

____

____

____

____

____

____

Appendix I
Speaking Feedback Form

This scale may be used to give feedback on any speaking activity in the book. It can be used by students or teachers.

Speaking Evaluation Scale	
Fluency Did the student speak at a natural speed with natural pauses?	/20
Pronunciation Did the student pronounce individual sounds correctly? Did the student speak with proper intonation, stress, and reductions?	/20
Grammatical Accuracy Did the student use the correct verb tenses? Were other structures used correctly?	/20
Content/Organization Did the student have interesting ideas? Did the student speak for a sufficient amount of time? Were ideas connected so that the speaking flowed smoothly?	/20
Vocabulary Did the student use an appropriate level of vocabulary? Did the student use any new words from the unit?	/20
General Comments **Total Points:**	/100

Appendix II
Irregular Verbs

BASE FORM	PAST FORM
beat	beat
begin	began
bend	bent
bleed	bled
blow	blew
break	broke
bring	brought
broadcast	broadcast
build	built
buy	bought
catch	caught
choose	chose
deal	dealt
draw	drew
drive	drove
fall	fell
feel	felt
fight	fought
find	found
flee	fled
freeze	froze
hang	hung
hear	heard
hide	hid
hold	held
hurt	hurt
keep	kept
know	knew
leave	left
lose	lost

BASE FORM	PAST FORM
mistake	mistook
pay	paid
quit	quit
read	read
ride	rode
ring	rang
run	ran
shoot	shot
speak	spoke
speed	sped
spend	spent
steal	stole
swim	swam
think	thought
throw	threw
understand	understood
upset	upset
wake	woke
wear	wore

The past form of some verbs can end in [ed] or [t]. Americans prefer the [ed] form.

BASE FORM	PAST FORM
burn	burned/burnt
dream	dreamed/dreamt
learn	learned/learnt
spill	spilled/spilt
spoil	spoiled/spoilt

Appendix III

Some Common Separable Two-Word Verbs

ask out
back up
bring up
call back
call up
cross out
do over
figure out
fill in
fill out
give away
give back
hand in/ turn in
hang up
leave out
look over
look up
pick out
pick up
point out
put away
put down
put off
put on
read over
start over
take down
take off
talk over
tear down
tear off
tear up
throw away
throw out
try on
try out
turn down
turn off
turn on
write down

Some Common Inseparable Two-Word Verbs

ask for
call on
come by
count on
depend on
do without
get in
get off
get on
get over
get up
give up
go over
go through
look after
look at
look for
look into
run into
talk about
wake up